YEMEN

Anna Hestler

MARSHALL CAVENDISH
New York • London • Sydney

Reference edition reprinted 2000 by
Marshall Cavendish Corporation
99 White Plains Road
Tarrytown
New York 10591

© Times Media Private Limited 1999

Originated and designed by
Times Books International, an imprint of
Times Media Private Limited, a member of the
Times Publishing Group

Printed in Singapore

Library of Congress Cataloging-in-Publication Data:
Hestler, Anna.
    Yemen / Anna Hestler.
        p. cm. — (Cultures of the world)
    Includes bibliographical references and index.
    Summary: Presents information about the geography,
history, government, and economy of this country located on
the southwestern tip of the Arabian Peninsula and describes
many aspects of the lifestyle of its people.
    ISBN 0-7614-0956-4 (library binding)
    1. Yemen—Juvenile literature. [1. Yemen.]
I. Title. II. Series.
DS247.Y48H46 1999
953.3—dc21   98-53993
                        CIP
                        AC

INTRODUCTION

VISITORS TO YEMEN are struck by how distinctive it is from the rest of the Arabian Peninsula. No wonder it is called the "green land of Arabia." Lush green valleys and rugged mountains stand in stark contrast to the endless deserts elsewhere.

Yemen's roots are far deeper than its Islamic past. Civilizations thousands of years old left remnants of impressive structures as a testimony to their genius. This was the fabled land of the queen of Sheba, where kingdoms flourished on the fringes of the desert.

In contemporary Yemen, ancient traditions survive in spite of modern developments spurred on by the recent discovery of oil. Yemenis still marry according to age-old customs, and tribesmen still wear handcrafted daggers. The unique Yemeni identity is alive and well.

CONTENTS

A Yemeni girl carrying a
bundle of qat ("kaht").

CONTENTS

A northern Yemeni boy wearing typical headgear.

GEOGRAPHY

YEMEN'S ARABIC NAME "AL-YAMAN" means southward (of Mecca). Yemen lies on the southwestern tip of the Arabian Peninsula. Its neighboring countries are Saudi Arabia in the north and Oman in the northeast. The southern shores meet the waters of the Gulf of Aden, a point of access to the Arabian Sea and the Indian Ocean. To the west, Yemen commands the straits of Bab al-Mandab ("gate of lament"), which is the narrow gateway to the Red Sea, the port of Jiddah in Saudi Arabia, and the Suez Canal. Across the straits are the African countries of Eritrea and Djibouti.

Yemen is about 214,230 square miles (554,856 square km) in area, slightly smaller than the state of Texas. Yemen's territory includes some islands. Socotra in the Arabian Sea, about 620 miles (1,000 km) east of Aden, is the largest, while Kamaran and the Hanish Islands in the Red Sea, and Perim in the straits of Bab al-Mandab, are slightly smaller.

Left: **The port of Aden is strategically positioned on the straits of Bab al-Mandab. That is why throughout history, foreign powers fought to control the city.**

Opposite: **A Yemeni proverb says, "Sana'a must be seen, even if the journey is long." Many have braved forbidding mountains and vast deserts to reach this "pearl of Arabia," the capital of Yemen.**

7

During the rainy season, flash floods caused this road to become an open drain.

LANDSCAPE

People often think of Yemen as yet another country on the Arabian Peninsula dominated by desert. However, in addition to the rich sands of the great Arabian Desert, the Yemeni landscape has remarkable features unusual on the Arabian Peninsula: beautiful coasts and sculpted peaks punctuated by valleys. There are no lakes or rivers, but dry riverbeds called *wadis* ("WAH-dees") filled with seasonal rains. These topographical differences have unquestionably contributed to regional variations in culture that have evolved over thousands of years.

Yemen can be divided into four regions: the coast or Tihama, the mountains, the Eastern Plateau and desert, and the islands.

THE TIHAMA, which means "hot earth," is a flat, narrow plain running parallel to the Red Sea. Across the water lies the eastern African shore, only 20 miles (32 km) away. Not surprisingly, as a result of the many cultural exchanges between the people of the Tihama and their African neighbors, similarities appear, such as the reed huts common to both areas. The sandy plain of the Tihama is 15–40 miles (24–64 km) wide. Irrigation has made parts of the plain fertile. The plain ends at rocky cliffs that are the edge of the Western Highlands. Over time, erosion of these cliffs has resulted in the formation of deep *wadis*. The southern coastal plain is dotted with volcanic rocks and is the site of the important port of Aden. Over countless years, Aden has acted as a doorway for trade and foreign influences.

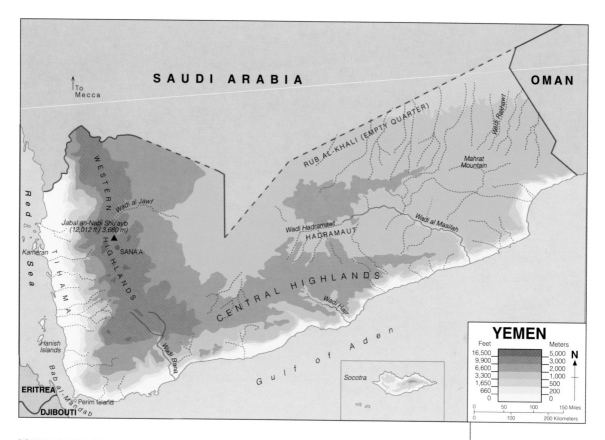

THE MOUNTAINS Mountain chains, known as the Western and Central Highlands, form the backbone of the country. Geologically, the Arabian Peninsula was once part of the African continent. Millions of years ago, a rift between the two created the Western Highlands. These mountains are made of lava and have stunning peaks that tower an average of 9,850 feet (3,000 m) above sea level. Yemen's highest peak, Jabal an-Nabi Shu'ayb, at 12,012 feet (3,660 m), is also the tallest peak on the Arabian Peninsula. Throughout history, highland people living in thousands of isolated villages perched on these craggy peaks have been cut off from outside influences. The peaks of the Central Highlands are slightly lower at an average height of 3,280 feet (1,000 m).

Cradled within the mountainous regions lie the country's fertile plateaus, the site of most of Yemen's urban centers, including the capital city, Sana'a.

Acacia trees in the Empty Quarter. The Empty Quarter makes up almost half of Yemen.

THE EASTERN PLATEAU AND DESERT The Eastern Plateau gradually merges with the vast sands of the Arabian Desert. The Rub al-Khali, which means Empty Quarter, lies between Sana'a and Saudi Arabia.

There is little permanent settlement in the desert, but it is the home of nomadic herders known as Bedouin, who roam across the desert in search of grazing land for their cattle.

Between the desolate hills of the Eastern Plateau and the desert, and running along the southern coastline, lies the Wadi Hadramawt, a place well known for growing dates. Located on a limestone plateau, it is just high enough to catch sufficient rain to cultivate crops. This *wadi* is one of the few areas in eastern Yemen fertile enough to cultivate.

THE ISLANDS Yemen has about 112 islands, including Socotra, Kamaran, Perim, and the Hanish Islands. Each island has distinct climatic, geographic, and environmental characteristics. Their geographic isolation from the mainland has enabled them to develop unique cultural traditions.

ISLAND OF SOCOTRA

In his book *Kings of Arabia*, written in 1923, Harold F. Jacob describes the people of Socotra: "On the coast these folk are of mixed Arab, Indian, African, and Portuguese descent, and they live mainly by fishing … In the mountains are … the true aborigines. These are light-skinned, tall, and robust, with thin lips, straight noses, and straight black hair."

Socotra, which means "island of blessing," is the most famous of Yemen's islands. It is mountainous, semiarid, and has an area of 1,197 square miles (3,100 square km). Every year for at least four months, the people on Socotra are isolated from the outside world because monsoon winds make it difficult for planes or boats to reach them. During this period, the islanders are self-sufficient. The island's economy is based on fishing and harvesting myrrh and aloe vera leaves.

Socotra is a botanist's dream because it has many rare plants, but many of them are threatened with extinction due to overgrazing. Some of them are renowned for their medicinal value, including the famous dragon blood tree which is used in oriental medicine to cure eye and skin diseases. In the past, the Chinese used it for dyes and in cinnabar lacquer for cabinets, and the medieval European scribes used it to make ink.

Socotra has many indigenous birds. The sun bird, grass warbler, mountain bunting, sparrow, and chestnut winged starling are just a few of the island's birds.

CLIMATE

As the most arable spot on the Arabian Peninsula, Yemen is often called the "green land of Arabia." After the rainy season, parts of Yemen look as though they are covered with a lush green carpet. The temperature varies with topography and elevation, but it is Yemen's mountains and location at the edge of the tropics that determine its climate.

Agriculture in Yemen depends on moist winds known as monsoons. When the monsoon winds blow from the south and southwest, the mountains trap the limited rainfall. During the rainy season, from April/May to July/August, the rains are very irregular, usually appearing as short, localized downpours. Torrential rains can wipe out a road in one village, while a neighboring village remains dry. The Wadi Hadramawt gets a sprinkling of rain, but the summer monsoons do not reach the Empty Quarter. Sometimes this area has no rain for years, making it virtually impossible to cultivate crops. Such unpredictable rains have challenged generations of farmers to build elaborate terraces and irrigation systems to trap scanty rainfall.

Yemen's regional climate varies considerably. The Western and Central Highlands are drier and cooler than the rest of the country. It has been said that the air is "as temperate and sweet as the fresh spring."

The winter season, from December to February, can get chilly though, with temperatures sometimes dropping below freezing. Cozy sheepskin jackets keep the highlanders warm during the winter.

Along the Red Sea and the southern coast, the climate is hot and humid. Temperatures can rise to 104°F (40°C) during June and July. To stay cool, people along the coast wear very loose clothes.

The desert and the Eastern Plateau are blisteringly hot. During the day, the temperature rises to 122°F (50°C), but drops as soon as the sun sets.

DUST STORMS

The *shamal* is a great dust storm that blows from the northwest across the Red Sea to the coastal areas of Yemen. It takes extremely high winds to create a dust storm. When the wind passes over areas of sparse vegetation, it picks up loose particles that can be as big as pieces of clay or as tiny as silt and fine sand. The particles are swept to heights of many feet, and the smaller ones can stay in the air for days—some of them have even been found floating in the atmosphere above Alaska. Heavier grains of sand bounce along the ground, just a few inches above the surface.

Sandstorms can be a real hazard. The sand particles carried by the wind act like sandpaper: they scrape away rock surfaces and remove paint from trucks. Dust storms can also erode valuable soil and destroy young crops.

During a *shamal*, the wind can become so full of sand that it blocks out the sun, making visibility impossible. Each year, airports have to close for a few days during the period of July and August because the *shamal* winds clog airplane engines.

Yemen lies on the same geographic latitude as the arid Sahel countries of Africa. There are periods of drought and poor harvests, but nothing like the famines of Africa. This is because the mountains trap rainfall, which can then be channeled for cultivation.

FLORA

In Yemen, there is a chewing gum tree. When the milky sap from the bark is left to dry in the sun, it develops a texture like gum. Passers-by peel it off and chew it.

Yemen's plants are fascinating and often exceptionally beautiful. In the Western Highlands there are flowering bushes of tamarisk, ficus, and acacia. The tiny yellow and white flowers of the acacia are often used for dyes. Fruit-bearing trees like mango and papaya, as well as Yemen's famous coffee shrubs, also grow well here.

The Central Highlands region has almond, peach, and apricot trees and a variety of grapevines that grow along its terraced slopes.

Farther east, parts of the desert have no flora. Among the plants that have adapted to this arid region is the useful aloe: the dried juice of its leaves relieves sunburn.

FRUIT OF THE DESERT

Throughout history, the date palm has played a vital role in the Middle East. It grows in areas where there is little water because it has long roots that can tap water sources far below the surface. In Yemen it flourishes around oases and in the Wadi Hadramawt. These trees can grow as tall as 92 feet (28 m). They start to bear fruit after four or five years and have been known to remain productive for up to 150 years. Each tree produces over 1,000 dates in a single bunch. Yemen's date harvest is for both domestic consumption and export.

Dates are tasty and nourishing. They are rich in iron, protein, fat, minerals, and other vitamins. Other than a source of food, the date palm has many uses: the trunks provide timber, the leaf ribs are used to make crates and furniture, and the smaller leaves are woven into beautiful baskets.

FAUNA

As recently as a century ago, Yemen had animals such as leopards, giraffes, pumas, oryx (large antelopes), and ibex (mountain goats). Sadly, the variety of wildlife has diminished because of hunting and population growth, which has resulted in the clearing of many natural habitats to make way for buildings.

Among the surviving animals are hyenas, wolves, hares, and foxes. The largest wild mammal still to be found in Yemen is the gelada baboon. The baboons scramble up the steep rock faces of the northwestern mountains, usually traveling in groups, and have been known to throw rocks at cars. Hamadryas baboons are also found in the mountains. They are occasionally kept as pets and taken to the local markets for shows.

Flamingoes frolicking in the coastal waters.

Despite the lack of animal wildlife, Yemen has plenty of birds: 13 species are native to the country, and 300 species of migratory birds stop in Yemen on their way to Europe and Central Asia. In the highlands there are ravens and vultures. Farther east, weaver birds build their nests on telephone poles.

Yemen also has a fair share of insects, spiders, and reptiles. Desert locusts live in areas where rainfall is erratic, but they travel en masse to search for food. Each year, swarms of desert locusts descend on the farms and within minutes, devour vital crops. Scorpions in the deserts and in some rocky parts of the highlands dart around grabbing small prey such as lizards. Desert reptiles, such as the desert viper, like to bask in the torrid heat of the desert, maintaining their body temperature by absorbing the heat of their surroundings.

CITIES

Yemen has thousands of small villages, and only about a quarter of the population is urban-based. As the economy grows and new industries develop, job opportunities attract rural migrants to the city centers. The main cities of Yemen are Sana'a, Aden, Ta'izz, and Hodeida.

SANA'A As the political capital of the Republic of Yemen, Sana'a is the largest and most important, as well as the oldest city in Yemen. The name Sana'a means "fortified place." At one time, the Sabeans, who ruled over one of Yemen's ancient kingdoms, used it as a highland fortress.

Sana'a is famous for its exquisite architecture and for its medina, the old walled center of the city. Many of the buildings in the medina are over 800 years old. But Sana'a is also a contemporary metropolis; it is this blend of ancient and modern that makes the capital so fascinating.

Since 1960 its population has doubled every four years. Its population now stands at approximately 472,200. Christians and Jews used to live in Sana'a, but today its residents are mostly Muslim Arabs.

ADEN (population: 270,000), built in the crater of an extinct volcano, is surrounded by huge lava mountains that shield the port from the elements, making it the best natural port on the Arabian Peninsula. Throughout history, Aden has been crucial to trade and transportation between the East and the West. After Yemen's unification in 1990, Aden was made the commercial capital.

TA'IZZ (population: 178,000), Yemen's third largest city, lies at the foot of Jabal Saber and sprawls over hills and lush green plains. The city is a thriving commercial center. Unlike other parts of the highlands, its markets have female merchants who are renowned for their great beauty and fierce bargaining skills.

Compared to Sana'a and Aden, Ta'izz is a young city. It has a modern appearance, since most of its concrete buildings were erected after 1962, the year the Yemen Arab Republic (YAR) was established. Despite its new look, some old quarters in the city and many lovely mosques remain.

HODEIDA In the 1960s the former Soviet Union modernized the city of Hodeida so that Soviet ships could make use of its port facilities. Since then, the city, which has a population of approximately 155,110, has continued to evolve, with concrete buildings and asphalt roads replacing the reed huts of local fishermen. The old Turkish quarter of the city remains intact, with handsome houses four stories high. The beautifully decorated doors of these houses were carved by Indian craftsmen who once accompanied traders to various ports.

Hodeida grew from a sleepy little fishing town to a major metropolitan city. Today, it is Yemen's second most important port.

17

HISTORY

ACCORDING TO ARAB TRADITION, around 2000 B.C., Semitic people, believed to be descendants of Shem, the son of Noah, made inroads into what is now northwest Yemen. They brought with them farming and building skills. About 1,000 years later, a great trading route developed. Caravans of camels laden with ivory, spices, incense, and textiles traveled through Yemen to the major markets of the ancient world.

The arrival of Islam in the 7th century was one of the most significant events in Yemen's history. Another historical turning point came much later, in 1990, when the northern and southern parts of the country merged into the Republic of Yemen. The period in between was marked by fighting between tribes and religious leaders, and against foreign invaders, including the British and the Ottoman Turks.

Above: **The ruins of the Ma'rib Dam are Yemen's most valuable archeological site. Built by the Sabeans around 500 B.C., this dam irrigated some 37 square miles (96 sq. km) of agricultural land that fed 50,000 people.**

Opposite: **Dar al-Hajar, a rock palace located in the Central Highlands. It was built in the 1930s by Imam Yahya as a summer residence. The government now owns this remarkable palace.**

PRE-ISLAMIC CIVILIZATION

The earliest known civilization in southern Arabia began about 1000 B.C., when kingdoms based on five city-states flourished on the fringes of the eastern desert: Saba (also called Sheba), Qataban, Hadramawt, Awsan, and Ma'in. Though still shrouded in mystery, each of these kingdoms appears to have enjoyed periods of prosperity, and they often coexisted. They also shared a similar faith based on polytheism, or the worship of many gods. The legendary kingdom of Saba, which lasted for at least 14 centuries, was probably the most powerful.

The kingdoms depended on agriculture and trade. Renowned for their brilliant building skills, the southern Arabians constructed ingenious dams and irrigation systems, enabling them to farm areas with little or no water.

19

The kingdoms became tremendously wealthy by trading with markets all over the ancient world. Southern Arabia was the source of two precious resins: frankincense and myrrh. Frankincense was burned as an incense offering to the ancient gods, and myrrh was an ingredient in cosmetics, perfumes, and curative treatments. These aromatics were highly valued by the ancient Greeks, Romans, and Egyptians. Besides trading their own goods, Yemeni merchants sold ivory from Africa, spices and textiles from India, and fine silk from China.

Goods were shipped from India and China across the Indian Ocean to the port of Aden. From there, camel caravans transported them along the Incense Road to the markets of Egypt, the Mediterranean, and Mesopotamia. So many riches poured out of southern Arabia at that time that the northerners called it "Arabia Felix," which is Latin for "Happy Arabia."

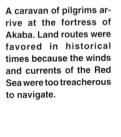

A caravan of pilgrims arrive at the fortress of Akaba. Land routes were favored in historical times because the winds and currents of the Red Sea were too treacherous to navigate.

THE QUEEN OF SHEBA

The kingdom of Saba is best known for its legendary queen of Sheba (Saba). The story of the queen's visit to King Solomon appears in both the Old Testament and the Koran. In the story a beautiful bird called a hoopoe brought news to King Solomon of the thriving kingdom of Saba and its queen. As queen of what may have been the most powerful kingdom in southern Arabia, she had great influence over the southern part of the Incense Road, while King Solomon controlled the northern end. Therefore, it was vital to cement friendly relations.

In order to do so, the queen and her entourage traveled by camel all the way to the court of King Solomon in ancient Palestine. On arrival, she presented the king with an abundance of gifts, including spices, gold, and precious stones. Her mission was so successful and the king so charmed that she became known as "Queen of the Arabs." This story has fascinated people of the East and the West ever since.

DECLINE OF THE KINGDOMS

In the first century A.D., when a Mediterranean seaman named Hippalus discovered a direct sea route between India and Egypt, the center of trade shifted westward to the coast of the Red Sea, where the kingdom of Himyar flourished. The caravan trails fell into disuse, and this loss of trade to India precipitated the decline of Saba. The whole of southern Arabia, including Yemen, became part of the Himyarite kingdom.

During the 4th and 5th centuries A.D., missionaries began converting the southern Arabian tribes to their own monotheistic faiths, and the old Sabean gods were forgotten. Around the same time, Christianity became the official religion of the Roman empire. Demand for frankincense and myrrh plummeted as the Christian Church associated their use with pagan rituals. Thus the kingdoms of southern Arabia lost much of their wealth.

In A.D. 525 the king of Ethiopia seized Yemen. Forty-five years later, he attacked the kingdoms of Arabia but failed to conquer the region. He died soon after. After his death the Himyarites enlisted the Persians' help to chase out the Ethiopians. Thus, when the Ethiopians were defeated in A.D. 575, the Yemeni kingdoms came under Persian rule.

Christian and Jewish influences entered southern Arabia on the trade routes and across the Red Sea from the ancient kingdom of Ethiopia. Christianity was Ethiopia's official religion.

This tomb honors the memory of Queen Arwa in a mosque in the town of Jibla (Ibb province). After her husband died in 1067, Queen Arwa ruled the Sulayhid dynasty (1046–1138), one of Yemen's medieval Islamic dynasties. This extraordinary and well-educated woman traveled widely in her state to encourage her people to abandon tribal quarrels and devote themselves to agriculture and development.

THE SPREAD OF ISLAM

By the early 7th century A.D., a new religion called Islam appeared on the Arabian Peninsula and was spread rapidly by an Arab prophet born in 570 named Mohammed. By 628, the Persian governor of Yemen had converted to Islam. Everyone in Yemen also converted.

After Mohammed died in 632, centuries of conflict followed, and a number of dynasties came and went. Among these were the Sulayhids, ruled by the exceptional Queen Arwa, and the Rasulids, who excelled in the arts and sciences.

The Zaydi (an Islamic sect) state in northern Yemen was established in 897 when a descendant of the Prophet was invited to mediate a war between two tribes, the Hashid and the Bakil. Imam Yahya bin Husayn bin Qasim ar-Rassi became the first political and religious ruler of the Zaydi dynasty. His teachings advocated an active political role for the *imam* ("ee-MAHM"), or religious leader, and emphasized the study of war. These principles laid the foundations of the Zaydi imamate.

THE EUROPEANS AND THE FIRST OTTOMAN OCCUPATION (1517–1636)

In the early 1500s, the emerging powers of Europe became more interested in the lucrative trade between the Far East and the Mediterranean. Their attention became focused on controlling the Red Sea and Arabian coastal ports, which were vital arteries of the East-West trade. The Portuguese were the first to arrive. They annexed the island of Socotra in 1507, and in 1513 Afonso de Albuquerque, the great conqueror of Goa in India, tried unsuccessfully to take the port of Aden. Spurred on by the Portuguese operations, the Mameluke rulers of Egypt mounted an attack on Aden, but failed.

By 1517 the Muslim Ottoman empire centered in Turkey had become the greatest military and naval power in the eastern Mediterranean and the Red Sea. In order to check Portuguese supremacy in the Indian Ocean, the mighty Ottoman Turks arrived in Yemen. They conquered Ta'izz, Aden, and finally Sana'a in 1548.

During the Ottoman occupation, trade with Europe grew, and a great interest developed in the precious coffee beans grown in Yemen's highlands. The port of Mocha on the Red Sea became a pivotal point in the world coffee trade, attracting the English and Dutch, who set up factories there.

Despite economic progress, the local population resented the occupation. As early as 1590, one of the Zaydi imams, Qasim the Great, challenged the Turks. The armies that finally expelled the Turks in 1636 were drawn from northern tribesmen and led by Qasim's son, Muayyad Mohammed.

Shaharah, a mountain town in northwest Yemen, can only be reached on foot. A narrow bridge over a chasm separates it from the next town. This near-inaccessible site was the ideal headquarters for the Zaydi imams in times of foreign occupation.

The British presence resulted in significant social changes. The number of Jewish, Christian, and Indian merchants in Aden increased, and indigenous traders were drawn from the interior of the country to a new way of life. As a result, Aden grew into a metropolis with a cosmopolitan population.

For more than 200 years, the Zaydi state extended its realm—east to the Hadramawt and as far north as the coastal region of Asir in modern Saudi Arabia. Centralized control fell apart when some groups began to claim independence. A turning point came when the Sultan of Lahej in the south blocked Zaydi access to the port of Aden in 1728. The British had been scouring the coastline for a coaling station en route to India, and this proved to be a golden opportunity for them to increase their influence in the area.

THE BRITISH IN SOUTH YEMEN

In the 19th century, a number of developments enabled Great Britain to expand its global realm. The development of the steam engine and railroads in the 1830s made transportation more efficient, and the ports of the Mediterranean and Red Sea became connected to the ports of London and Liverpool in England. With the increasing activities of the British East India Company, Aden became an important port of call for ships and steamships on the route between Europe and India.

In 1839 the British took over Aden. It was ruled by British India until 1937 when it became a British crown colony. To protect Aden from a Turkish takeover, the British drew up a number of protection treaties with the local sheikhs, or tribal leaders. In return for British military protection, the sheikhs promised not to transfer their territory without British consent. In this way, Great Britain's South Arabian Protectorate was formed.

Under British rule, the port of Aden took on a new size and importance. It benefited from political stability, improved commercial policies, and updated harbor facilities. Aden became a center for the transshipment of goods and a hub of trading activity, surpassing the traditional ports on the Arabian and Red Sea coasts.

THE SECOND OTTOMAN OCCUPATION (1849–1924)

In the mid-19th century, the Ottoman Turks reappeared as a major influence in the Red Sea region. This event led to a Turkish takeover of north Yemen. They began by reestablishing their authority in the Tihama region in 1849, in order to forestall British control of the entire Red Sea. The opening of the Suez Canal in 1869 prompted the Turks to expand into the highlands. They occupied all the major cities, until finally they captured the Zaydi capital of Sa'da in 1882.

Eventually Ottoman and British interests clashed. Both powers agreed to demarcate boundaries between them, and drew a border between north and south in 1905. This sealed the division between north and south Yemen, a division that lasted until unification in 1990.

The local population opposed the Turkish occupation, and there were a number of uprisings by the Zaydis as well as the northern Tihama tribes under the leadership of Sayyid Mohammed al-Idrisi. In 1904 Imam Yahya ibn Mohammed organized a resistance movement among the highland Yemenis. Under the 1911 Treaty of Da'an, he finally forced the Turks to accept a division of power granting him autonomy in the highlands.

After Turkey's defeat in World War I in 1918, the Turks withdrew from North Yemen. The Treaty of Lausanne officially ended Turkish rule, and North Yemen obtained international recognition as an independent state ruled by Imam Yahya. South Yemen remained in the hands of the British.

This magnificent Turkish mausoleum in Ta'izz was built during the Ottoman empire.

CONSOLIDATION OF THE ZAYDI IMAMATE

After gaining independence, Imam Yahya set about consolidating central authority and securing the borders. In the Tihama, in 1925, he conquered the Idrisi forces, who then allied themselves with Saudi Arabia. Yahya's northern advances alarmed the Saudis, culminating in the Saudi-Yemeni War of 1934. This ended with the Ta'if Treaty, leaving Asir and Najran temporarily under Saudi rule. These territories are still in dispute today.

Fearing that outside contact might result in challenges to his authority, Imam Yahya decided on a policy of isolation. His efforts were aided by North Yemen's agriculturally self-sufficient economy. At a time when the rest of the Arab world was modernizing, Yemen turned inward.

Nevertheless, Imam Yahya realized that to be secure, he needed foreign technology, particularly military, and this required education and training. In the 1930s the first Yemenis left to be educated abroad. Once exposed to foreign ideas, however, they began to question his leadership. In 1948 a group of liberal reformers, led by Abdullah al-Wazzir, assassinated Imam Yahya, but his son, Imam Ahmad, drove them out. Later, he established his own government, which closely resembled his father's.

SUPERNATURAL POWERS

Imam Ahmad had tremendous personality—he was shrewd, well-educated, amusing, suspicious, and often terrifying. He dealt severely with dissidents and was feared by his subjects, who believed that he possessed supernatural powers. The imam played upon the public fear of his alleged psychic powers by making it known that he communicated with the spirit world. His servants claimed that they could hear him talking to the jinn (spirits) when he was alone in his room. His subjects also believed he possessed power over poisonous snakes that warned him of plots threatening his life. Imam Ahmad's efforts to cultivate a fear of his power did not deter the hostile forces against him, which included some tribal chiefs and members of the intelligentsia.

FORMATION OF THE YEMEN ARAB REPUBLIC

Following Imam Ahmad's death in 1962, his son Mohammed al-Badr came to power. Within a week, a group of army officers staged a coup, deposed him, and proclaimed the Yemen Arab Republic (YAR) with Colonel Abdullah Sallal as president. Imam al-Badr fled to the northern mountains and organized forces to help him restore his regime. The country plunged into civil war. Egypt and the Soviet Union supported the republicans, while Saudi Arabia and Britain backed the imam's royalists.

By 1967 the fighting had reached an impasse. The royalists faced defeat, and internal conflict troubled the republican ranks. As a result, the Egyptians withdrew their troops, and President al-Iryani replaced President Sallal. The civil war finally ended in 1970 when Imam al-Badr was exiled to Britain. The republicans established a new government that lasted until 1974 when a group of army leaders took control of the government and steered the country in a conservative direction.

Imam al-Badr (above) had only been in power for a week when his confidant and bodyguard, Colonel Abdullah Sallal, swept him off his throne.

President al-Shabi (right) signs the independence agreement with Lord Shackleton of Britain. The president had demanded £100 million as reparations for 128 years of colonial rule. The British conceded only a small amount, which dashed all hopes of rebuilding the country.

THE PEOPLE'S DEMOCRATIC REPUBLIC OF YEMEN

The 1960s were also turbulent times for South Yemen. Despite opposition, in 1963 the British created the colony of Aden to be included in the Federation of South Arabia. Although Britain promised to grant independence to the federation at a later date, nationalism had already swept through the south. Among the nationalist groups a left-wing rebel movement known as the National Liberation Front (NLF), was organized and began a campaign of terror in 1963. The federation finally collapsed in 1967, forcing the British to withdraw. The NLF declared South Yemen independent. In 1970 it became the People's Democratic Republic of Yemen (PDRY) under the leadership of President al-Shabi. Eventually the NLF developed into the Yemeni Socialist Party (YSP).

The economy of the new republic was a shambles. The closure of the Suez Canal in 1967 aggravated the effects of the loss of British trade and investment and further reduced Aden's economic role in the world. The country managed to stay afloat only with financial aid from the Soviet Union and other communist countries of Eastern Europe.

To make matters worse, an internal ideological power struggle threatened the country's political stability. Political sentiment became more left-wing and even more closely allied with the communist bloc. In 1969 President al-Shabi was ousted in favor of President Salim Rubayi Ali, who brought most of the economy under government control.

UNIFICATION OF THE TWO YEMENS

At the beginning of the 1970s, both the YAR and the PDRY relied on foreign aid to revive their war-damaged economies. Saudi Arabia and Europe supported the YAR, while the PDRY was aided by the Soviet Union. Strained relations resulted in a series of wars along their border.

In 1978, after a succession of leaders, Colonel Ali Abdullah Saleh became president of the YAR. He embraced a Western-style market economy. During the 1980s the economy grew stronger under his rule.

Meanwhile, in the PDRY, a civil war broke out in 1986 when the views of extreme Marxists clashed with those of the government. Around the same time financial aid dried up with the collapse of the Soviet Union. Bankrupt, the PDRY turned to its neighbor for help.

Previously there had been unification talks between the two Yemens, but the discovery of oil in the desert bordering both countries sped up the process. They finally merged in 1990. Saleh became president, and a southerner, Ali Salim al-Baydh, became vice-president.

The first few years for the new nation were filled with trouble. A disagreement between supporters of the president and those of the vice-president resulted in a civil war in 1994. But within a few months, troops supporting the president won the war, and the country remained united.

During the 1990–91 Gulf War, the Yemeni government wanted Iraqi troops to be withdrawn from Kuwait and Western forces from Saudi Arabia because they felt "an Arab problem" needed "an Arab solution." This infuriated the Saudis, who sent over 600,000 Yemeni workers home.

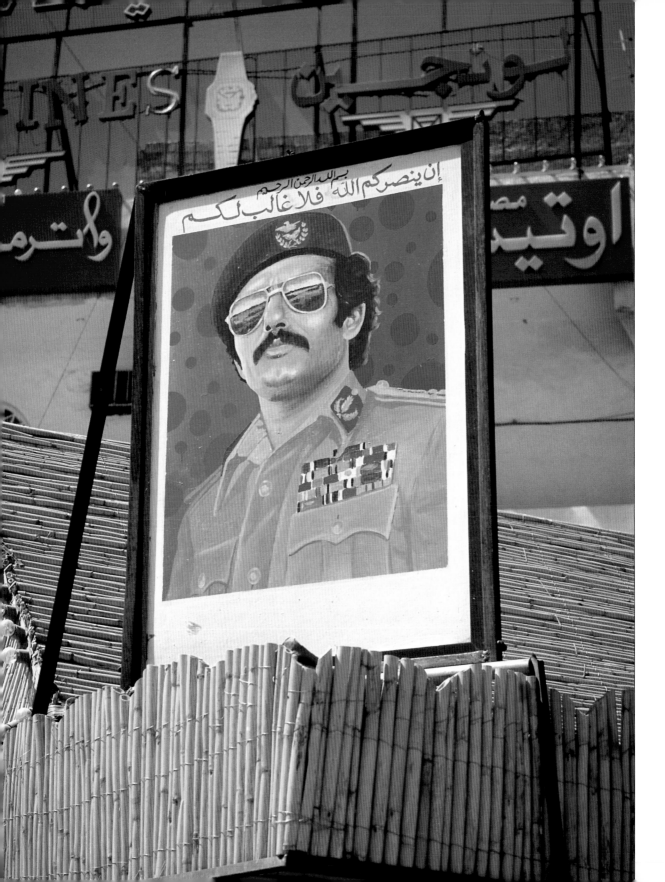

GOVERNMENT

THE FORMATION OF THE REPUBLIC OF YEMEN on May 22, 1990 was one of the most momentous occasions in the history of Yemen. At last, the people of both Yemens had become part of one nation.

Yemen's political system is unique on the Arabian Peninsula. The people wanted a democratic system of government based on direct popular elections, freedom of speech, and an independent judiciary. The struggle for democracy came from the people's desire to end absolute rule.

THE CONSTITUTION

Before unification, the two Yemens had different political systems. North Yemen was a republic, ruled under a provisional constitution dating back to the 1970s, although successive governing bodies exercised little real power until the 1980s. In contrast, the PDRY favored Marxist principles; government policy was determined by the Yemeni Socialist Party.

Left: **People stop to look at the Liberation Monument in the middle of Revolution Square.**

Opposite: **A poster of the president of Yemen, Lt.-Gen. Ali Abdullah Saleh. He has been in office since 1978.**

Once the two Yemens had agreed to unite, the legislatures of both the YAR and the PDRY approved a draft constitution for the new nation. This constitution was a major deviation from the previous two. Despite opposition from certain factions, the majority of the population supported the constitution in a popular referendum in mid-May 1991. Yemen was governed by this constitution until October 1, 1994, when some amendments were made.

The revised constitution defines the Republic of Yemen as "an independent and sovereign Arab and Islamic country." It states that the republic "is an indivisible whole, and it is impermissible to concede any part of it. The Yemeni people are part of the Arab and Islamic nation." The revised constitution stipulates that *Shari'ah* ("SHAHR-i-a"), which is the Islamic law, is the source of all law.

A further amendment abolished the five-member presidential council, which included the president and the vice-president. Today, the president is in a stronger position because the people elect him directly.

Opposite: **Bedouin boys march down the streets.**

OPPOSITION TO THE CONSTITUTION THWARTED

Not everybody embraced the original constitution wholeheartedly. Among those who opposed it were religious groups in the north, including the Muslim Brotherhood. They objected strongly to the proposed constitution and urged the rest of the population to boycott it, because it was not based exclusively on Islamic law.

In the south, there were demonstrations by women. Afraid that their freedom might be jeopardized if Islamic sentiments became too extreme, they demanded that their rights be guaranteed in the new constitution.

All objections were thwarted when the leaders of both Yemens proclaimed unification on May 22, 1990, six months ahead of schedule. The Republic of Yemen was born with Sana'a as its political capital and Aden as the economic center. President Saleh was selected to lead the people into a new era.

THE INSTITUTIONS OF GOVERNMENT

The constitution set out a parliamentary system of government based on direct popular elections. Anyone who is above 18 years of age can vote. The Council of Representatives (Parliament) is the legislative branch of the state, and its 301 members are elected for a four-year term. The Parliament is responsible for enacting laws, approving policies and development plans, supervising public spending, and ratifying international treaties. The president cannot dissolve the Parliament, except in an emergency.

The president and a cabinet of ministers make up the executive branch. The president is elected every five years, and his term may be renewed only once. He is empowered to appoint the vice-president, prime minister, and other ministers on the advice of the prime minister.

The issue of local government is still under discussion, but Yemen is currently divided into 17 administrative units known as governorates, sometimes called provinces. Headed by governors, these governorates are divided into smaller units known as districts and local councils. The local government administers various aspects of community life, such as health, education, and tax collection.

A sentry guard at the entrance to Sa'da. There are about 42,000 men in the armed forces in Yemen. Besides an army, a navy, and an air force, there is also a paramilitary force with an estimated 50,000 members.

THE LEGAL SYSTEM

The principles of Islam concern all aspects of life, and Islam provides its followers with a means of ordering their daily lives according to the will of Allah (God). Muslims believe that God's words were revealed through the Prophet Mohammed, and later became the Koran, the holy book of Islam. These sacred writings were supplemented by a collection of Mohammed's sayings known as the *Hadith* ("ha-DEETH"). Together, they form the basis of *Shari'ah*, or God's Way, which is the law of Islam. *Shari'ah* includes a range of rules governing behavior. These include religious rituals such as prayer, family matters such as marriage, and how a Muslim should behave in society. In addition to *Shari'ah*, the tribes have their own unwritten customary laws relating to standards of good behavior and social conduct.

The state and the judiciary are separate within Yemen's legal system. This means that judges can carry out their duties independently, and the courts have the power to decide all disputes and crimes. The law is the only authority that governs their work.

The structure of the courts is consistent with the administrative divisions of the country. Every district has a court of first instance, which tries civil, criminal, matrimonial, and commercial cases. Every governorate has a court of appeal that looks into appeals against the decisions of the district courts. The Supreme Court, located in the capital city of Sana'a, is the highest court in the land. Headed by a chief justice, with a bench of seven judges under him, the Supreme Court looks into appeals against decisions of the courts of appeal.

POLITICAL PARTIES AND CIVIL WAR

Following unification, over 40 new parties vied for popular support. Yemen became the first multiparty state on the Arabian Peninsula. The first election, held in April 1993, drew enthusiastic voters. The result was a three-party coalition: the General People's Congress (GPC), formerly dominant in the north; the Yemeni Socialist Party (YSP), formerly dominant in the south; and the Islah party, which represented tribal or Islamic interests.

Soon after the election, clouds began to gather. A disagreement over the sharing of power between the GPC, led by President Saleh, and the YSP, led by Ali Salim al-Baydh, pushed the country to the brink of disaster in 1993. A full-blown civil war broke out on May 4, 1994.

Shortly after the war began, al-Baydh proclaimed the independent Democratic Republic of Yemen, hoping to win the support of those countries on the Arabian Peninsula that did not support Saleh. However, Saleh's troops surrounded Aden, and the secessionists, including al-Baydh, fled to other parts of the Arab world.

After the YSP's defeat, President Saleh affirmed his commitment to democracy. To prevent future uprisings, he declared that party membership would no longer be allowed within the armed forces. To foster reconciliation, most secessionists who put down their weapons were granted amnesty. Despite its brevity, the civil war was a blow to the fragile economy and tipped the political balance of power. The YSP lost influence and a coalition between the GPC and Islah ruled until April 1997, when the GPC won a majority. Since then, the government has assumed more influence over the opposition and the media.

This damaged South Yemeni Russian tank is a painful reminder of the last civil war. The cost of the civil war was tremendous: thousands of people lost their lives or were wounded, and the economy was crippled. After the war, water and electricity were in short supply, and the price of basic foodstuffs and fuel skyrocketed.

The Islah party, which was formed in 1990, has two branches: tribal and religious. Islah's political focus is on the relationship between Islam and the state, and the issues of religious education.

Female students having a discussion. Behind them is the University of Sana'a.

ISLAH'S WOMEN

There is quite a female force behind Islah, Yemen's largest Islamic party. Although Islah does not have any female candidates, women work behind the scenes to help the party. They come from varied backgrounds, but quite a few are university graduates. Most of them are in their late teens or early twenties and do not have any children yet. All of them are extremely religious, and they consider the work they do for the party their religious duty.

Islahi women are involved in a number of social activities that bring them into daily contact with other women in society. There are religious study groups, women's committees, women's centers, charities, and various other women's groups. Many of these activities are just part of the Yemeni way of life, but they provide Islahi women with an opportunity to educate other women about the Islah party in order to gain their support. In the course of their daily contact with other women, Islahi women have contributed to the success of the Islah party.

POLITICAL OUTLOOK

In recent years, President Saleh has remained steadfast in his efforts to rectify economic conditions and improve foreign relations. The international community supported his government's implementation of an economic reform program and rewarded it with aid. Nevertheless, the austere economic policies have resulted in domestic protests. In particular, the removal of energy subsidies, which increased the price of fuel, resulted in a confrontation between the army and farmers.

In 1992 tensions between Yemen and Saudi Arabia increased because of a dispute over an oilfield near the Saudi-Yemeni border. Both countries agreed to negotiations in mid-1992. Since then, relations have become more amicable and Yemen and Saudi Arabia have expressed their commitment to improving economic, commercial, and cultural cooperation. In June 1995 President Saleh made a successful visit to Saudi Arabia. He has been working ever since to improve relations with the rest of the Arab world and with Western countries. Yemen is a member of the United Nations, the Arab League, and the Organization of Islamic Conference.

The Hashid and Bakil tribes are the most prominent in Yemen. Many tribesmen hold important positions in the government, and a number of tribal sheikhs are unofficial government employees who receive salaries and cars. President Saleh is a member of a Hashid tribe near Sana'a.

PRESIDENT SALEH

President Saleh was born in 1942 in the village of Bait al-Ahmar in the Sana'a governorate, where he attended a Koranic school for his elementary education. In 1958 he joined the armed forces and to continue his studies, enrolled in the noncommissioned officers' school in 1960.

President Saleh has a long and successful military career in which he was promoted through the ranks. He attended various service schools, assumed a number of posts, and in 1983, attained the rank of colonel. Today, as president of the Republic of Yemen, he is commander-in-chief of the armed forces.

ECONOMY

THROUGHOUT HISTORY, most Yemenis have been farmers. In modern times, Yemen's economy has been largely dependent on foreign aid and the wages sent home by Yemenis who work in other Arab countries. Since the discovery of oil in the 1980s, earnings from oil production and the Aden refinery have significantly contributed to Yemen's income.

THE CHALLENGE OF DEVELOPMENT

With unification, Yemen inherited two opposing economic systems. The former YAR operated a Western-style economy with very little government interference. The PDRY was centrally planned—its government decided how and what to produce, and who would receive the goods. Both had similar economic traits, however—inward-looking and reliant on foreign aid and remittances from Yemeni workers abroad. After unification, the YAR system was adopted.

To get the economy back on its feet, the government, with the help of the International Monetary Fund (IMF) and the World Bank, began implementing an ambitious program of economic reform in 1995.

Left: **An oil tanker berths at the Aden refinery jetty. With the help of foreign companies, oil production in Yemen is now about 365,000 barrels per day.**

Opposite: **Selling incense in the market. Yemenis like to burn incense at home because burning incense gives off a pleasant fragrance.**

Modern machinery is used on large farms but this farmer still uses the traditional method of plowing.

AGRICULTURE

Rain is the source of life in Yemen. It enables crops to flourish on about 25% of the land: the Tihama coastal plains, the highlands, and the eastern provinces of Ma'rib, Al-Jawf, and the Hadramawt valley. But the rains are temperamental, challenging farmers to construct ingenious irrigation systems to catch the water. The highlands are covered with exquisite terraces that prevent fertile soil from being washed away. Some farmers now use diesel pumps to run water to their fields, so when fuel prices were raised, there was a public outcry.

Although declining, agriculture is still the primary occupation of 60% of the population. Ironically, this agrarian society accounts for only one-fifth of the total goods and services produced in Yemen. Households farm small plots of land, thus they produce very little. Each year fewer people farm, and less is produced.

Yemen, once self-sufficient in food, now depends on imports. One reason is that the opportunity to work for wages abroad or in the cities has become an attractive alternative to working in the fields. This reduces the labor force available for farming and therefore leads to less produce. On the other hand, the resulting income has helped to diversify the economy. When the men return to their villages, some of them have saved enough money to open shops. Other enterprising men invest in a truck and shuttle villagers back and forth for a fee.

Another reason is that more qat, a shrub whose leaves are chewed for their stimulating effect, is being grown at the expense of food crops. A great deal of controversy surrounds this crop. Although women chew qat, it is more prevalent among the men. Many men spend a large portion of their income and a fair amount of their time chewing qat. This habit used to be confined to the rich elite, but it became affordable to the rest of society when incomes rose. Because of the high local demand, a large number of farmers have converted their land to qat fields.

This is a qat field in the highlands near Sana'a. Qat is the Yemeni substitute for alcohol. When chewed for a long time, it induces a state of happiness comparable to the effects of alcohol.

Coffee is native to north Yemen, Kenya, and Ethiopia. All three countries have similar flora and fauna because they were part of the same land mass until a rift created the Red Sea.

MOCHA COFFEE

Only 200 years ago, Yemen supplied all of Europe with coffee. It was shipped from the port of Mocha, hence the name Mocha coffee. Even after competitors entered the market, coffee remained Yemen's primary source of foreign exchange. Since the 1970s, however, coffee production has been declining because more farmers are growing qat.

But coffee could make a comeback. In Western markets, the name Mocha is associated with good coffee. It has a strong aroma and is perfect for blending with other beans and coffee lovers are fond of the delicious Mocha-Java combination. Attempts to boost coffee production began in the 1980s, with a ministry of agriculture development project designed to discover how to increase the yield per acre. Although African and Latin American plantations can produce cheaper coffee, Yemen has a competitive advantage when it comes to the taste.

Yemen's agricultural output is quite varied. It includes grains such as sorghum, corn, wheat, barley, and millet, and vegetables such as radishes, onions, beans, lentils, and leeks. Fruits include mangoes, bananas, apricots, and grapes from the Central Highlands, while the Hadramawt grows dates for export. North Yemen is renowned for its honey and Mocha coffee. Nonfood crops include qat, tobacco, and cotton.

Most rural families breed livestock for milk and meat. Women herd cows, and children tend sheep and goats, which provide wool and hides. In recent years, farmers have also been rearing chickens in commercial farms as the demand for eggs has grown.

WOMEN IN AGRICULTURE When men left for better-paying jobs abroad or in the cities, some of them were able to send enough money home so that women could purchase appliances in order to lighten the house-keeping load. Still, many rural women carry an extra burden. A rural woman is up at the crack of dawn, cooking for the family and feeding the animals. She might have to collect firewood or fetch water, a backbreaking task when it involves a climb into the mountains. Then she tackles the farm work—sowing seeds, weeding fields, spraying pesticides, plowing, and harvesting. Even old women perform some light tasks. For those whose everyday chores are heavy, there is less free time available for them to do the things they enjoy. A number of government projects are now in place to help women produce more with less effort, so that they can have more free time even as they increase their income.

The *suq* ("SOOK"), or market, is a place where goods and services are exchanged. Since most markets are only held once a week, market day is the highlight of the week for most people. They arrive early on foot or by truck to get the best products ranging from fruit and fabric to television sets and cars. Women do not usually go to the *suq*. In Yemen it is usually the men who shop.

NATURAL RESOURCES

Rich fishing waters around Yemen are the most undeveloped natural resource. The Red and Arabian seas are full of mackerel, squid, shrimp, lobster, cuttlefish, and tuna. Most fishermen are small-scale entrepreneurs who lack the money to buy more efficient equipment. Even if more fish are caught, there are insufficient processing plants to turn fish into a valuable export.

The discovery of oil reserves in the 1980s brightened Yemen's economic prospects. Commercial extraction began in 1986. Oil wells were opened and pipelines were built to transport the oil from the fields to the coast.

Yemen mines substantial quantities of salt and marble. Because the country's unique architectural styles require cement, stone, alabaster, and marble, local demand for these commodities is very high.

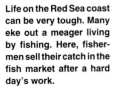

Life on the Red Sea coast can be very tough. Many eke out a meager living by fishing. Here, fishermen sell their catch in the fish market after a hard day's work.

INDUSTRY

There are few factories in Yemen, and the industrial sector accounts for only one-fifth of national output. Oil refining is the most important industry. The construction industry is growing, along with the manufacture of bricks, tiles, and other building materials. Other manufactured goods include processed food, bottled soft drinks, cigarettes, aluminum houseware products, and rubber and plastic products.

The service sector, mainly government and trade services, accounts for half of Yemen's national output. Public service, distribution, packing, shipping, insurance services, and tourism are expanding.

As in most developing countries, Yemen's industrial development is constrained by a shortage in factors of production: supplies of water and energy are unreliable and the local work force lacks industrial expertise. The transportation network is inefficient, with no guarantee that goods are delivered to the industries and markets on time.

In the 1980s, there was such a shortage of building blocks that some thieves resorted to raiding archeological sites.

TOURISM

Yemen has a lot to offer the tourist: a good climate, stunning landscapes with untouched beaches, scuba-diving sites, a cultural heritage with fabulous architecture, and no shortage of historical sites to explore. Yemeni hospitality is unmatched and their customs are fascinating.

The possibilities to develop tourism are endless. The government plans to modernize business and tourist facilities such as hotels, convention centers, and restaurants, and to encourage foreign and local investment. With sufficient funds and appropriate government guidance, tourist revenue could be a significant source of income.

One obstacle to the growth of tourism is kidnapping. Some foreigners who have strayed from the beaten track have been kidnapped by tribesmen, who use the hostages to increase their bargaining power with the central government. Some of these victims are treated rather well and plied with local drinks and delicacies.

A truck journeys across the desert. Although all the major towns and cities are now paved with roads, thousands of miles of tracks between them are barely passable by all-terrain vehicles.

ENERGY AND TRANSPORTATION

Every business and household needs power. It takes energy to run a machine, switch on lights, use an electric blender, or turn on the television. In Yemen there is not enough energy to go around, so it is expensive and supplies are unreliable. Locally produced petroleum meets some energy requirements, but the country is still reliant on imported fuel and energy. Until the 1960s Sana'a had no electricity, but now nearly everyone has it. Supplying electricity to some remote rural areas is costly, so these areas have to be supplied by local generators.

Inadequate power supply is a problem that the government is trying to solve. There are plans to use more natural gas for power, and money is being channeled into small electric power projects in rural areas.

Yemen is more accessible than it ever was, although it lacks railroads. Prior to 1960 nearly all roads were earthen tracks, suitable only for donkey-drawn carts or four-wheel drive vehicles. A journey must have seemed endless. Great strides have been made since then and the quality and quantity of roads connecting agricultural and industrial centers have improved. While only 8% of the road network is paved, this is quite an achievement for a country with such rough topography.

Ships from many countries visit Yemen's ports; the two main ports are Aden and Hodeida. Docking facilities have improved in the last decade, and Aden is on the way to reestablishing itself as a center for international trade and shipping. There are six airports, and international travelers can fly directly into Sana'a, Ta'izz, Aden, and Hodeida. Yemen Airways is the biggest airline in the country, and flies nearly all over the world.

TRADE

Yemeni goods used to travel to nearly every corner of the world, but nowadays there are more imports than exports.

Trade flowing into the country includes essential foodstuffs and goods necessary for economic growth. Food, consumer goods, machinery, equipment, vehicles, pharmaceuticals, chemicals, and petroleum products come from North America, Western Europe, and Japan. There is a ban on fruit and vegetable imports to protect local farmers. Crude oil, coffee, salt, cotton, dates, and salted fish are exported to North America, the Arabian Peninsula, Japan, and China. The United States is Yemen's biggest trading partner.

Yemen's imports include electrical appliances. In 1997, the value of imports exceeded the value of exports. This trade deficit is offset by remittances from Yemenis working abroad and by monetary transfers from Saudi Arabia.

The Central Bank of Yemen, established in 1971, is responsible for issuing currency and managing the government's foreign exchange and other financial operations.

FINANCE

Yemen's unit of currency is the riyal (YR), and its value against other currencies determines how affordable imported goods are. In 1995 the riyal was devalued, probably because the government wanted to make exports cheaper in order to reduce the trade deficit. This made imports expensive and the country could not afford to import the machinery and equipment needed to develop the economy. Since then, the value of the currency has stabilized.

While the government has put its finances in order, it still spends more than it earns. With economic reforms, government revenues are rising and the budget deficit has declined. Deficits used to be met by printing more money, which led to inflation. This made it expensive to buy the most basic items. Since 1996 the central bank has promoted economic growth by trying to keep down inflation. Systems for collecting revenues, such as taxes and customs duties, have been strengthened, and earnings from crude oil exports have helped. However, the government cannot count on oil to fill its coffers, since the world market price for crude oil is dropping.

In order to develop the economy and improve the well-being of the people, Yemen needs foreign aid. This money, in the form of loans or grants, comes from international donors like the International Monetary Fund, the World Bank, the European Union, and the United Nations. In 1998, Germany and the Netherlands decided on a three-year increase in aid, which will be used to improve health, education, roads, and water supplies, and to develop agriculture. Foreign investment is also encouraged, and there should be more incentives for investors in the future.

THE ENVIRONMENT

As in other countries, economic growth has been at the expense of the environment. Land has been farmed and animals hunted to the extent that most of the natural flora and fauna have been destroyed. When laborers migrated elsewhere for work, they abandoned terraced fields, and it took only a few years to wash away fertile soil from neglected fields.

A recent development is the shortage of water. As more pumps are used for irrigation and household use, the level of ground water is sinking. In many areas, access to fresh drinking water is limited, jeopardizing the health of the population. Fortunately, a water resource program is being developed with the help of international donors.

Oil production and tourism also pose some environmental problems, but they are not major problems yet. There is a chance that proper planning can prevent further environmental degradation.

There is very little rain in Ma'rib. Even when it rains, the water evaporates very quickly. In order to extract water, people dig very deep holes. These are lined with pipes that are connected to pumps at ground level. Here, a camel pulls a primitive pump to draw up water.

YEMENIS

THE MAJORITY OF YEMENIS are Arabs, yet there is an extraordinary diversity among them. There are variations in religious affiliation between regions, among tribes, and within society. Underneath it all, the Yemeni people are straightforward, kind, full of life, and down to earth.

POPULATION

With a population of nearly 17 million, Yemen is the most populated area on the Arabian Peninsula. The majority of Yemenis live in small villages scattered across the countryside. Another 23% live in cities or towns, and this is increasing as the country develops.

The population is growing fast, at an annual rate of 3.8%, as the average woman bears about seven babies during her lifetime. In the early 1990s, when the men returned from the Gulf region, the population peaked.

Left and opposite: **There are many young people in Yemen. Over half of the population is under 15 years old.**

THE ARABS

The majority of Yemenis are Arabs, but they divide themselves into two genealogies based upon their ancestors. The first group, the southern Arabs, are sons of Qahtan (from the Biblical Joktan) and originated in Yemen. Qahtan was the son of Shem and the grandson of Noah. The Hashid and Bakil tribal groups trace their ancestry from Qahtan and are said to be related to the ancient Sabeans. The second group, the northern Arabs, are the sons of Adnan and originated in northern Arabia. Adnan is the Islamic version of the Biblical Ishmael, one of Abraham's sons. Sayyids, who are members of Yemen's religious elite, are northern Arabs. Historians confirm that both groups have been in Arabia from the earliest known times.

Throughout most of their history, the Arabs of the interior have not been exposed to intruders because the desert and sea kept out foreign influences. There is more racial mixing in the towns and seaports. For example, some of the people living along the Red Sea are of African/Arab descent.

Like other rural children, this Tihama girl helps to take care of the family cattle.

YEMENI JEWS

The number of Jews in Yemen is certainly not reflective of their importance. For centuries, the Jews were the largest non-Muslim group living permanently in Yemen. Most of them are descendants of the indigenous people who adopted Judaism in pre-Islamic times, so Jewish Yemenis and Muslim Yemenis look alike.

THE BEDOUIN

The Western perception, largely influenced by Hollywood, of the traditional Arab is of the Bedouin—camel-breeding tribes who roam the deserts. But the majority of the tribes in Yemen are not nomadic; they are sedentary cultivators. Only about 1% of the population are Bedouin, and they are concentrated in the eastern governorates, especially al-Mahra. Of course, this is just an estimate, since it is difficult to get an accurate census of nomads.

The Bedouin have always been fiercely proud of their freedom and ability to survive with the bare necessities: their livestock, a tent, a rug, and a few cooking pots. Despite their remarkable independence, they have never lived in total isolation. Throughout history they have sold their thoroughbred camels to villagers and townspeople and have purchased those items that they could not produce themselves, plus a few luxuries such as tobacco.

Today many Bedouin have settled or gone to work in the oilfields. Others still lead a more traditional lifestyle, but the tracks of four-wheel drive vehicles that cut through the desert are telltale signs of change.

The innovative spirit of the Yemeni Jews had a major impact on the indigenous non-Jewish culture. When they departed, many traditional crafts disappeared.

Under the Zaydi imams, the Jews were a protected group. Although there were restrictions on their lives, they were accepted as part of the social order. Many were employed as merchants, money-changers, and craftsmen. The Yemeni Jews were very innovative. The beautifully handcrafted Yemeni silverware best displays their talents.

With the spread of Zionism, a movement that sought to establish a Jewish state in Palestine, more and more Jews began emigrating. When the State of Israel was founded in 1948, the Jews left in droves. Almost half of the population in Sana'a used to be Jewish. Today, there are just a few thousand in the whole country, living in mountain villages.

SOCIAL STRUCTURE

Yemenis have traditionally been stratified by descent, distinguishing those of religious status from the tribal farmers and those who worked in the marketplace. In theory these status distinctions are a relic of the past, but nevertheless, they still exist.

At the apex of the social pyramid are the Sayyids, who are descendants of the Prophet Mohammed. During the Zaydi imamate, they held important government positions and were wealthy landlords. Because of their education, religious knowledge, and administrative expertise, Sayyids are respected to this day. Quite a number of them are teachers, healers, and mediators in tribal disputes. Another elite group are the Qadis ("KAH-dis"), Islamic scholars of law, who are usually of tribal ancestry. Their status is hereditary, and a number of great Qadi families have played important roles in Yemen's history, such as President al-Iryani of the former Yemen Arab Republic.

Tribal people of Qahtani ancestry fall below the elite groups and are farmers. A tribal unit is headed by a sheikh, who is a wise man of good character. He oversees village affairs and may sometimes act as a government official. The members of a tribe have a strong sense of

belonging, and each tribe has its own characteristic dress, poetry, dance, and cuisine.

Below the tribal people are those members of society of unrecognized descent. They have many different names that describe their origin or their occupation. These people perform various services—they may be butchers, barbers, or wedding musicians. Sometimes they are called Bani Khums ("BAHNI-hums"). A popular myth about the origin of the Bani Khums is that they are related to a sheikh who shamed his tribe, and whose children were forced to become servants.

At the bottom of the social pyramid are those who perform menial jobs like sweeping the streets. In the past, these people were social outcasts.

In recent years, people's attitudes are changing, and as a result the traditional social hierarchy is weakening. With the emergence of a market economy, the occupations given low status, such as the services performed by the Bani Khums, have become more respected. In addition, education is no longer confined to the elite members of society. Therefore, literacy is slowly moving down the social pyramid.

Above: **Male villagers stand united with their sons. Behind them is their village.**

Opposite: **A man adorns himself with a rifle and** *jambiya* **("JAHM-bi-yah"). These weapons are carried more as status symbols than for self-defense in Yemen.**

RURAL/URBAN DIVISIONS

The division between the rural and the urban population is as important as social distinctions. The tribal people are rural folk who work in the agricultural sector, while the Sayyids, Qadis, and others employed in trade, commerce, or manufacturing perceive themselves as city folk.

There is a bit of good-natured competition between the urban and rural people. The tribal people consider city folk to be weaker and less healthy, and some city folk consider the rural people to be less sophisticated. But these differences will become less pronounced as mobility increases.

MEN'S WEAR

The old saying "you are what you wear" is certainly descriptive of traditional male attire. Clothing identifies where a man comes from, his

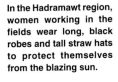

In the Hadramawt region, women working in the fields wear long, black robes and tall straw hats to protect themselves from the blazing sun.

tribe, and his position in society. The type of headgear and the way it is worn, and the appearance and position of his dagger are important too.

Traditional male tribal dress consists of a *futa* ("FOO-ta"), which is a wraparound skirt, a handwoven turban, and a *jambiya,* which is a ceremonial dagger. The dagger is worn upright and center, and kept in place by a leather or cloth belt. You can tell which tribe a man belongs to by the way he wraps his turban around his head. In addition, he might wear a short coat made of woven wool, or a sheepskin. A shawl thrown over the shoulders serves to keep him warm, and can also be used as a handy tote bag.

Today, dress patterns are changing. In the cities, more men are wearing suits and ties. Traditional clothing is often combined with Western-style shirts and blazers, and colorful imported cloth covers the head. Tribal dress has also become fashionable among nontribesmen.

Two men in traditional dress. Their headgear, as well as clothing, identifies their clan loyalties.

WOMEN'S DRESS

Yemeni women are striking and have a real talent for draping head coverings and veils. The regional variation in clothing styles is fantastic; rural and urban women dress very differently.

Most women wear leg coverings such as bloomers, slacks, or tights under their dresses. For special occasions such as religious festivals and weddings, women wear their loveliest outfits and traditional jewelry. Glittering silver adorns neck, ankles, wrists, and sometimes the forehead.

Since Yemen is a Muslim country, the women dress modestly and tend to veil themselves in the presence of strange men. The outer head coverings among urban and rural women are different. Rural women may wear one or more scarves on their head and a woolen shawl for weddings, or when traveling beyond their village. These shawls are placed on the head in a variety of interesting shapes and can enhance their femininity.

In the Tihama, many women are not veiled. They wear hats woven from palm fronds, resembling those worn in Mexico. Women in the mountains drape sprigs of sweet-smelling basil over their ears for decoration or to protect against the evil eye, or evil spirits.

Most urban women wear a face veil and are frequently enveloped in a *sharshaf* ("SHAHR-shahf"), which is a loose, black garment that covers the body, or are gracefully attired in a *sitara* ("SEE-tahr-a"), a brightly colored covering.

The colors that the women wear are different from region to region. In Sana'a, many women wear bright cloths imported from India. Women from the Tihama region dress in colorful garments, and in eastern Yemen, women working in the fields wear black robes.

Opposite: **In accordance with Islamic rules, many Yemeni women cover themselves with veils and robes.**

BODY PAINTING

Despite the influx of European cosmetics, women and girls still paint themselves with traditional makeup for special occasions. Before a religious festival, women will paint black floral designs on their hands and feet with a substance called *khidab* ("KAY-dab").

In Sana'a, it is customary for a bride to be embellished by an experienced body painter before her wedding. The ink is applied to the body with a needle, an acacia thorn, or even a toothpick. The face and neck are decorated while the arms are decorated from the hands to the shoulders and the legs from the feet to the knees. Although there are catalogs containing various patterns, an experienced body painter uses her imagination to create vivid designs. This ritual takes several hours and a lot of patience, but it makes a beautiful bride!

LIFESTYLE

YEMENI FARMERS, herders, fishermen, and professionals all lead very different lives. In the rural parts, daily life is physically strenuous. In the city, amid the hustle and bustle, people from all kinds of backgrounds intermingle. In spite of their differences, a similar set of values regulates their lives: living in a group (be it family, tribe, or village) is more important than living alone.

SOCIAL VALUES

A Yemeni's allegiance is first to the family and then to society. Most responsibilities are shared among relatives, friends, and neighbors. When someone goes on a trip, a neighbor might take care of essential tasks such as tending the livestock. If anyone is missing from a gathering, a friend or neighbor will drop by to ensure that everything is all right. When two people are arguing in the street, a bystander may step in to mediate.

Left: **Motorcycles are very highly prized in Yemen. These men are showing off their treasured possessions.**

Opposite: **A Yemeni man enjoying a smoke.**

Friends often gather for breakfast at a coffee stall. Such socialization is an intricate part of Yemeni life.

Two of the Yemenis' most delightful traits are their hospitality and generosity, especially toward guests and those less fortunate. Perhaps the queen of Sheba started the tradition of hospitality when she showered King Solomon with gifts.

A guest is honored and welcomed as though part of the family. The host will do just about anything to ensure that visitors feel at home, plying them with plenty of food, drink, gifts, and entertainment. This warm-hearted generosity is not just confined to the home. For example, when a Yemeni is eating in front of another, he or she will always offer to share the food.

THE PACE OF LIFE

Human relationships are extremely important in Yemen. Whether in a mountain village or in the city, people always have time to exchange a smile and a greeting. In the villages, people live in close proximity, especially those in the mountains where the houses are huddled together.

There is plenty of social interaction, as daily chores are rarely performed in isolation; there is always time to chat with one's neighbors.

In the cities, life is faster, more cosmopolitan, and less personal. Yet people still approach their work in a different way compared to most urban Westerners. When conducting business, some time is always devoted to exchanging family news, and the common phrase *"insha' Allah"* ("EEN-sha Allah"), which means "God willing," reveals the Yemeni attitude that time and deadlines are flexible. In both the cities and the countryside, men and women get together (in separate groups) in the afternoons to sip tea, chew qat, and chat. A number of city offices close for these afternoon gatherings.

Yemeni men spend a lot of time chewing qat because they believe it can give them strength.

THE FAMILY

A Yemeni family may consist of a whole collection of relatives who live under the same roof. Nobody lives alone. Grandparents, widows, and divorcees are all taken under the family wing. However, the number of family members living under the same roof is decreasing. Some men move into their own house when they marry. This gives the new wife more freedom to run her own household.

There is a prescribed order regulating family life. Each family member has a specific role and responsibility based on their age and sex. For both men and women, authority is based on seniority. The elderly command the utmost respect, and their opinions are highly valued. They are often asked to mediate in disputes.

The head of the household is the father who provides for his family. He has the last word on all matters. A mother raises the children and takes

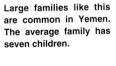

Large families like this are common in Yemen. The average family has seven children.

care of household chores, although she may not be strictly confined to this role.

The men generally assume tasks that require contact with the public, such as shopping in the market for household provisions. Women cook, clean, and do the washing. Younger and fitter women also do the more strenuous work, such as carrying water and fetching fuel.

CHILDREN

To the Yemenis, children are gifts from God and welcomed after marriage. Due to limited hospital facilities, many women deliver babies at home, assisted by an older female family member or a midwife.

A large family is highly valued in rural areas because there will be more people to help with the many chores. Children have to help look after their younger siblings, and to harvest the crops. However, these days it is harder to make a living from the land and more women choose to have smaller families so that they can afford to educate their children for non-agricultural jobs.

A proud father shows off his son. Yemeni parents love their children dearly.

Yemeni parents are proud of their children and raise them in a loving environment. Girls are taught to be patient, loving, modest, and helpful. Boys learn that they must protect the women of their family and uphold the family honor. The children also pick up other skills required for an urban or rural life from their parents, grandparents, and older brothers and sisters. In cities, boys may learn how to conduct a business deal or ride a motorcycle while girls may learn how to operate modern cooking appliances. In rural areas, boys may learn how to operate or repair a diesel pump while the girls learn how to sew and cook.

ARRANGED MARRIAGES

A Muslim man is permitted to marry up to four women, provided he can care for them equally. In practice, most Yemenis have only one wife.

Most marriages are arranged by the families of the prospective couple, but they are rarely forced. Since Yemen is an Islamic country, there is greater segregation of the sexes. In a small town a young man might know a girl by sight but he would have few chances of meeting the girl. Therefore, he relies on the advice of his mother or sister who knows the women of the neighborhood well.

Once a mother has decided on a girl based on her dignity and status, she confers with her husband. If both parents agree on their choice, they consult their son. After a prospective wife has been chosen, father and son pay a visit to the house of the bride's family to speak to her father. However, the decision is not made right away. The potential father-in-law has to think it over and discuss the matter with his daughter. Only when everybody agrees is a date fixed for the betrothal.

The betrothal is quite an informal affair. Father and son, along with a few male relatives, deliver a number of gifts, such as raisins, dates, clothes, and qat, to the bride's house. They also give the engagement ring to the girl's father for safekeeping. Then they discuss suitable dates for the wedding and agree on a bride price, which is usually paid in cash. At this point, the couple are officially engaged, and the wedding plans begin.

EDUCATION

Until the 1960s formal education was primarily the privilege of the elite members of society. Many children were schooled in the village mosque where instruction was oral and the emphasis was on memorizing the Koran rather than learning to read and write. A lucky few went to Aden or Egypt to be educated, but many children remained illiterate.

Today everyone has a right to an elementary education, which is free and compulsory. Children start elementary school at 6 years of age and finish at 15. After this, some children continue their studies in secondary school until the age of 18.

More Yemeni children are able to read and write than before, but there is still a gap in literacy between girls and boys. In addition, getting to school is more difficult for children who live in remote rural areas than for those in urban centers because of inadequate transportation.

For the minority who pursue higher education, there are modern universities and a number of vocational training centers. At the university in Sana'a, students can choose from a number of degree programs: arts, science, medicine, law, commerce, and education. The extended family comes in handy for young mothers, enabling them to continue their studies as everybody pitches in to look after the children.

Until the early 1990s, only a quarter of all females in Yemen attended school. After the unification, a new constitution was passed stating the right of all citizens to an education. More girls now have the opportunity to pursue higher education.

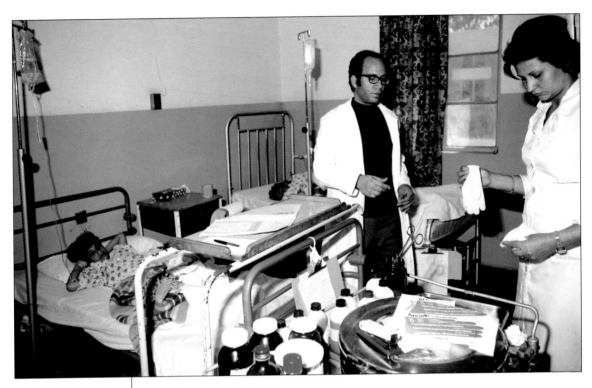

HEALTH

Yemen has a long tradition of folk medicine. There are healers throughout the country with their own special herbal remedies to cure ailments and diseases. A well-known folk remedy is barberry, used to alleviate internal bleeding and stomach problems. Sadly, some of this folk wisdom is not passed on, nor is it being incorporated into modern medical practices.

Some Yemenis believe that there are evil or mischievous forces that can cause sickness. Charms, amulets, and plants are used to control these forces. One important plant is rue, an evergreen shrub. The leaves of the rue are worn to ward off the evil eye. Words are also thought to be curative and it is not uncommon for Koranic verses to be recited over a sick person.

Modern health services are being developed, but there are still not enough doctors or hospital beds. One obstacle to providing proper health facilities is that many people are scattered in small villages. The shortage of drinking water and poor sanitation contribute to diseases such as tuberculosis and typhoid.

ANCIENT MEDICINE

There is an ancient body of medical literature in Yemen. Some of this knowledge is based on Greek medical research, where the core belief was that the human body consists of four elements: earth, fire, air, and water. The combination of these elements in a person's body is supposed to give them a particular "temperament," and one has to balance these elements in order to stay healthy.

A distinctive Islamic medical tradition grew out of these principles and built on the practices of Prophet Mohammed and his companions regarding health and sickness. These practices stressed the importance of fresh air, exercise, and diet. The Rasulids developed a body of sophisticated medical literature on herbs, surgery, diseases, magical treatments, and preventative diet. The importance of eating different foods during different months and seasons was emphasized. For example, hot, fatty foods were to be eaten in October, while cold, wet foods, such as fish and sour milk, were recommended for June.

INSIDE A TOWER HOUSE

A tower house is a multistoried house with many attractively decorated rooms. Each family unit has its own room or story, while certain communal areas are shared. The ground floor is usually used for storage. Families live on the upper stories where there are bedrooms, sitting rooms, dining areas, kitchens, and bathrooms.

People often sleep in different rooms depending on the season, occupying the warmest ones in the winter. Old people are given light and airy rooms to make them more comfortable. The rooms are usually furnished in the same way: a chest or a trunk for a person's personal items and some wooden pegs for hanging clothes.

The best room in the house, the *mafraj* ("MAHF-rahj"), is also the highest. It is therefore perfect for enjoying a view of Yemen's dreamy landscapes. The walls are often whitewashed and decorated with delicate patterns and verses of poetry. The floor may be covered with mattresses, carpets, and decorative cushions. This is where socializing, entertaining, and other leisure activities take place. Afternoons are spent here eating snacks, chewing qat, listening to music, and exchanging the latest news.

Male strangers are supposed to stay out of the areas used by women. If they have to pass the women's quarters on the way to the *mafraj*, they call out "Allah Allah" to announce their approach, so that the women can shut their doors or cover their faces.

Yemenis were already inoculating themselves with the blood of smallpox survivors long before Westerners developed this technique.

RELIGION

ISLAM WAS BORN in the same area as the religions of Christianity and Judaism. The followers of all three faiths share the same God, the main difference being their understanding of his prophets or messengers.

Islam is a religion and a way of life that transcends the differences among the people of Yemen and binds them into one brotherhood. Islam is the official religion, but there are also some Christians and Jews.

THE PROPHET

The Arabic word for God is Allah and the word Islam means recognition of and submission to the will of God. A follower of the Islamic faith is called a Muslim. Muslims are found all over the world. They may be Arabs, Indonesians, Indians, Africans, Americans, or other nationalities.

Muslims believe that their religion is based on revelations from God. Like Christians and Jews, Muslims believe in the prophets of the Bible, and accept that Jesus was a great prophet, but not the son of God. Islam teaches that Mohammed was the last messenger of God and his teachings are the most precise revelations from God.

Mohammed was born in Mecca, an important trading and cultural center in Saudi Arabia, in A.D. 570. As a boy, Mohammed already disliked the beliefs of his fellow Arabs. When he was older, he became a traveling merchant. He was successful but disturbed by the greed around him, so he often retreated to the mountains to think. At the age of 25 he married a noblewoman, Khadija, and they had six children.

At the age of 40 a profound experience changed his life. According to Islamic tradition, the angel Gabriel appeared to Mohammed one night, and for over 20 years thereafter, communicated God's words to Mohammed. These revelations concerned issues of religion, government, human conduct, and relationships.

Allah has 99 beautiful attributes including "the Gracious, the Merciful, the Compassionate, the Kind, the All-Knowing, the All-Wise, the Lord of the Universe, the Creator ..."

Opposite: **A Muslim studies the Koran in the Great Mosque of Sana'a.**

71

Encouraged by his wife, Mohammed began preaching to the people of Mecca, urging them to abandon the idols they worshiped and lead better lives. The establishment in Mecca first became concerned, and then hostile as Mohammed's following grew. Mohammed and his followers fled north to Medina in A.D. 622. This became known as the *Hijra* ("HICH-rah") or the year of migration, and year one of the Islamic calendar.

In Medina the Muslim community continued to grow stronger. By A.D. 630 they had conquered Mecca.

SUNNISM AND SHI'ISM

When Mohammed died in A.D. 632, Islam had been accepted by the majority of the Arabs. After his death, one of his close friends, Abu Bakr, was chosen to lead the Muslim community. Some time after Abu Bakr's death, when a group called the Shi'a refused to accept one of the later successors, a major split began to develop within Islam. The division between Shi'ism and Sunnism remains to this day. The Shi'a believe that Muslim leadership should be descended from Ali, Mohammed's cousin and son-in-law, because they consider Ali to be the first spiritual leader. The Sunnis, who are considered to be more traditional and orthodox, believe that elected members of the Muslim community can become leaders. Both divisions agree on most of the major matters of faith and worship, but some of their laws are different.

Within Shi'ism and Sunnism, there are different sects. About one-third to one-half of Yemen's population are Zaydis, a Shi'a sect. The Ismailis, another Shi'a sect, make up about 1% of the population. The rest of the population are Sunni Muslims who belong to the Shafa'i sect.

This Ismaili man belongs to the Shi'a sect, which expanded into Yemen from eastern Arabia and Egypt in the year 1061.

THE KORAN AND THE HADITH

The Islamic faith is based on the Koran—a book of God's words spoken through Prophet Mohammed. Muslims accept the Bible but believe the Koran is the supreme source of divine instruction.

The Koran is divided into 114 *suras* ("SOO-rahs") or chapters, which have different verses. Muslims try to memorize as many verses as they can.

The life of Prophet Mohammed embodied the teachings of the Koran and is therefore another source of guidance. Many of his sayings were memorized and preserved by his companions. The *Hadith* is a collection of these sayings. It instructs Muslims on daily activities, such as washing before praying.

A number of events and people mentioned in the Bible are also found in the Koran: the Creation, the Flood, the Exodus, Abraham, Moses, David, Solomon, and Jesus are some of these.

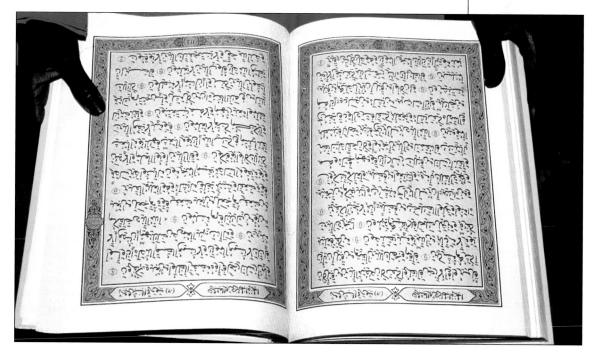

THE FIVE PILLARS OF ISLAM

Besides accepting Islam's beliefs, a Muslim must fulfill five religious duties. These duties play an important part in maintaining a sense of belonging to the Muslim community. They are known as the "Five Pillars of Islam."

1. SHAHADAH ("sha-HAHD-a") is confession and the essence of a Muslim's faith. It involves reciting two statements: "There is no God, but God," and "Mohammed is the prophet of God." Muslims repeat these statements daily in prayer. The belief that Mohammed is God's last and ultimate messenger distinguishes Islam from Judaism and Christianity.

2. SALAT ("sa-LAHT") is prayer. A Muslim must pray five times a day, at sunrise, midday, mid-afternoon, sunset, and at night. Prayers can be performed anywhere—at school, at work, at home, outdoors—but there is a prescribed form. Before praying, Muslims must be in a state of mental and physical purity. They first gargle and spit to cleanse their mouth. Then they wash their face, neck, hands, arms, and feet.

Praying involves reciting parts of the Koran, bowing, kneeling, and touching the head to the ground, symbolizing submission to God. Some

PURIFICATION

A fundamental requirement of Islam is ritual purity. A prayer has no value unless one has purified oneself in mind and body beforehand. According to the Koran, water is the beginning of life and is used for purifying the body. Wherever there is water, there is usually a place of prayer. In the highlands of Yemen, worshipers gather around streams and ponds to make their ablutions and pray. In the cities, worshipers frequently purify themselves in bathhouses. Almost every mosque has an ablution pool. However, throughout the Arabian Peninsula, water is not always easy to come by. In such cases, the worshiper can make the ablution with sand or simply go through the motions with the hands.

Muslims kneel on a prayer rug as they pray. While praying, Muslims face the direction of Mecca, the spiritual center of Islam. Mecca is the place where the central shrine of pilgrimage for Muslims, called the Ka'bah, lies. The Ka'bah is a small stone building that houses the Black Stone. Muslims believe that this stone fell from Paradise when Adam and Eve were cast out.

Opposite: **Archeologists believe these pillars in Ma'rib are part of a temple called Bilqis, consecrated to the moon god. According to legend, anyone who stayed within the temple walls was protected from his pursuers.**

According to Islamic tradition, all Muslims should give alms before the end of Ramadan. Alms-giving is supposed to purify the giver's soul.

3. ZAKAT ("za-KAHT") is alms-giving. According to the Koran, one is supposed to give up one's "surplus." So the third pillar involves giving a certain percentage of one's wealth to the poor and needy.

4. SAWM ("sa-AHM") is fasting. All Muslims are expected to go without food or drink during the daylight hours of the month of Ramadan. Everyone is required to fast except small children, the elderly, or the infirm. Those traveling may refrain from fasting, but they make up the days at a later date. The pace of life practically comes to a standstill during Ramadan, and many shops stay closed until after the midday prayers. Muslims believe that during Ramadan the gates of paradise are opened and the gates of hell are closed, and the sins of those who fast will be forgiven. This is a time of religious contemplation. Muslims stay up late at night to read the Koran and visit the mosque more often than usual. At the end of the month there is a great festival with rich food and presents. This is known as *Eid al-Fitr* ("id ul-FIT-r"), which is a celebration of the breaking of the fast.

5. HAJJ ("HAHJ") is pilgrimage. At least once in a lifetime, Muslims who can afford it should travel to the holy city of Mecca. The pilgrimage represents an act of obedience to God and should be made in the 12th and last month of the Islamic year. *Eid al-Adha* ("id ul-ah-DAH"), or the feast of the sacrifice, marks the last day of the pilgrimage, which lasts 10 days.

Each year millions of Muslims from all over the world travel to Mecca. The pilgrims wear simple white robes that make it impossible to distinguish the rich from the poor. They are symbolic of the Islamic belief that all men are equal before God. Pilgrims do not wear perfume or jewelry. They must abandon any vanity and seek forgiveness, guidance, and salvation from God.

RITES OF THE *HAJJ*

The *hajj* is not just a trip to Mecca. Numerous rituals must be performed and Muslims prepare themselves by studying these under a religious leader. At a certain point on the road to Mecca, pilgrims must purify themselves, don the *hajj* garments, and proclaim their intention to make the pilgrimage. Upon arrival, they pray at the Great Mosque and walk around the Ka'bah seven times, touching or kissing the black stone. Afterwards, they visit other holy sites in the vicinity.

Some of the other rites include running between the hills of Safa and Marwa; drinking from the well of Zamzam to commemorate Hajar's (one of the Prophet's wives) desperate search for water for her baby; and standing for most of the day in meditation at the Mount of Mercy (Mount Arafat), where Mohammed gave a famous sermon. On the way back to Mecca, Muslims stop at Mina to perform another symbolic act known as "stoning the devil." Small stones about the size of peas are thrown at pillars that represent the temptations of Satan.

The pilgrimage concludes with the sacrifice of an animal, usually a sheep, goat, or camel. To signify the successful completion of the *hajj*, the ritual ablution involves snipping a few locks of hair and trimming the nails.

In the past, the *muezzin* called Muslims to prayer from the top of a minaret. Today, the call is usually recorded and broadcast over loudspeakers.

THE MOSQUE

When Mohammed and his followers arrived in Medina in A.D. 622, there was no suitable place where they could worship. Therefore, they gathered in Mohammed's house to listen to his sermons and to pray. His house became known as a *masjid* ("MAHS-jid"), which is Arabic for mosque. This is a place of prayer and worship, as well as a place of rest and study.

Traditional mosques are rectangular and built of brick or stone or whatever material is locally available. There is a slender tower from which the *muezzin* ("MWEHZ-in"), or mosque official, gives the call for Muslims to pray.

Mosques have similar features. There is a courtyard with a place for worshipers to wash and leave their shoes. Inside the prayer hall is a special niche in one wall indicating the direction of Mecca. There is also a pulpit for the prayer leader.

The prayer hall is a single large room with carpets for worshipers to kneel on. There are usually other rooms for study groups.

Many mosques are richly decorated with geometric designs and verses from the Koran. There are no religious scenes of God or Mohammed because Islam forbids the use of graven images.

A man praying in the courtyard of the Great Mosque.

PRAYER AND DAILY LIFE

Muslims divide their day according to the five obligatory prayer times. At dawn, the *muezzin* makes the first call to prayer.

The first person to wake rouses the rest of the family. Once out of bed, the men, often clad in the same white robes worn as nightshirts, will set off for the mosque. The women usually pray in the privacy of their home. After morning prayer, the daily routine begins. Children get ready for school, the women begin the day's cooking, and the men (if they work, the women too) get ready for work.

When the sun reaches its peak, the *muezzin* calls the faithful for the midday prayer. After prayer, family members meet for lunch and then return to their daily activities.

When the sun is at a 45-degree angle to the earth, it is time for the afternoon prayer. Some men resume their work after this, while others get together to chew qat and discuss the events of the day. The women also have gatherings where they exchange news. The sunset prayer signals that it is time for the women to return to their homes. After the sunset prayer the family eats supper. There is a little time for homework, watching television, or listening to the radio until the evening prayer. Then it is time for bed.

الرّجاء من الأخوة سائقي
السيارات عدم إزعاج النزلاء
من خلال استخدام المهون
او زيادة دون السيارة ..
وخاصة في الفترة الصباحية

Drivers Are Gently Re-
-quested . Not To Dist-
-urb Our Guests Thro-
-ugh Using Horn Or Tn-
-crease The Motor Acc-
-elerator Particularly
In The Morning Time .

LANGUAGE

ARABIC IS ONE of the most expressive languages in the world. The written word is beautiful and the spoken word is musical. The Arabic language occupies a special place in the hearts of its speakers because it is the sacred language of the Koran. Yemen is one of many nations using Arabic.

THE ARABIC LANGUAGE

Broadly speaking, Arabic belongs to the Hamito-Semitic family of languages. More specifically, Arabic belongs to the Semitic group of languages and is closely related to Hebrew, the language of the Jews. Semitic people are descendants of Shem, the son of Noah. Two thousand years ago, Arabic was first spoken by the people living on the Arabian Peninsula.

Nobody is quite sure how the language developed, but the Arabs have a myth about the origins. According to tradition, God put the Arabic language in Adam's mouth at the time of Creation. When Adam disobeyed God, he was forbidden to speak Arabic and had to learn Syriac instead.

With the expansion of Islam, the Arabic language spread to other parts of the world. From its birth place on the Arabian Peninsula, Islam spread east and west from A.D. 600 to 900. At its zenith, the Islamic empire and the Arabic language extended from Spain across North Africa, and through the Middle East to Central Asia and India. Today, over 120 million people speak Arabic. It is the official language of many countries in north Africa and the Middle East.

Top: **These Himyaritic writings were engraved on the stone of the old Ma'rib Dam in 600 B.C.**

Opposite: **Warning signs in English and Arabic, like the one shown here, make Yemen a friendlier place for tourists.**

81

Taking photographs of Yemeni women and children without their permission could lead to ugly consequences: fights, police intervention, and confiscation of cameras.

LETTERS AND NUMBERS

The Arabic alphabet was probably invented in the 4th century A.D. It has 28 characters and is written and read from right to left. There are no capital letters, but the shape of a letter changes depending on its position in a word. The Arabic script has a rich variety of forms and makes for magnificent calligraphic decoration. The ancient Kufic script, which is heavy and angular, was used in the earliest copies of the Koran.

Many English words come from Arabic, including alcohol, algebra, checkmate, lute, magazine, and zero. Nevertheless, writing Arabic words into English is complicated. Many of the sounds used in Arabic have no equivalent in the English language, and most vowels are not written. Therefore, an Arabic word can be rendered in English in a variety of ways. For example, both "Muslim" and "Moslem" are perfectly legitimate, as are "Muhammad," "Mohammed," and "Mehemet."

Even the numbers that we use today come from the Arabs. Long ago, the Christian world used Roman numerals, where letters represent numbers. For example, the letter C is 100, and the letter M is 1,000. Therefore, the figure 2,500 would appear as MMCCCCC. The numbers, 0, 1, 2, 3, 4, 5, 6, 7, 8, and 9, which are so familiar to us, are known as Arabic numerals. The symbols for all these digits, except zero, originated in India around 200 B.C. The zero was developed only after A.D. 600. The word *zero* is probably the Arabic version of the Hindu word *sunya*, which means "empty." Traders and merchants introduced this Arabic number system across the Mediterranean and into Spain. From Spain, it spread throughout Europe.

WRITING

The language used for writing throughout the Arab world is known as Classical Arabic. It is an ancient language, modeled after the language of the Koran. Classical Arabic has changed very little over the centuries.

Poets and writers used Classical Arabic in the early Islamic period. It is considered the most eloquent form of Arabic. As the sacred language of the Koran, all Muslims, regardless of their native tongue, perform their recitations in Classical Arabic because they believe that to translate the words of God into another language would be impious.

Classical Arabic is a difficult language to read, even for those who speak it. Moreover, it lacks certain vocabulary necessary in today's world. As a result, a simplified version of Classical Arabic, known as Modern Standard Arabic, has developed in the last century. It is much easier to read and allows for the expression of modern concepts. Children in all Arab countries learn to read and write Modern Standard Arabic, and it is the language of radio, television, novels, films, and legal documents.

Looking surprised at the photographer's curiosity, a Yemeni schoolboy displays his handwritten exercise in Arabic.

THE ANCIENT SABEAN SCRIPT

Many alphabetic scripts used along the Mediterranean coastline are traceable to the Phoenician alphabet of about 1000 B.C. The Phoenician script was an advancement from the pictorial script used by the Egyptians. It was spread by Phoenician sailors and merchants who traded their goods with the peoples of the eastern Mediterranean. Hebrew and Aramaic evolved from Phoenician.

Although the history of writing is not entirely certain, it appears that two variations of the Phoenician script, known as the North and South Arabian scripts, were being used on the Arabian Peninsula around 500 B.C. The South Arabian script was also called the Sabean script, named after the legendary kingdom of Saba. Thousands of Sabean inscriptions carved in stone or engraved on rock faces or bronze statues have been discovered in many parts of south Arabia. The Sabean script is also found in some of the earliest Ethiopian inscriptions. With the decline of the kingdom of Saba, the script fell into disuse, and the Arabic used today did not come from the Sabeans.

SPEAKING

Although the Arabs share a common written language, variations in the spoken word have evolved over time. Today, spoken Arabic, also known as Colloquial Arabic, consists of four dialects: Syrian, Arabian Peninsula, Moroccan, and Egyptian. Some of these are mutually unintelligible; although two literate Arabs can communicate by using Classical Arabic, most Yemenis would find it difficult to converse with a Moroccan. Local dialects also vary within a country. In Yemen certain Arabic letters are pronounced differently in the north than they are in the south.

The Arabic language is an emotional one and has a powerful effect on its users. When reciting poetry, chanting the Koran, or giving a speech, Arabs will often get carried away. The words and sounds of Arabic have a richness that evokes great feeling. Arabs love the harmony of word combinations, and concern themselves more with the impact of words than with their meaning. They are inclined to use sonorous words to express themselves. Because of the nature of the language, there is a tendency toward exaggeration, repetition, and the use of metaphors and similes, which produces an even stronger effect. The words of an articulate speaker can leave an audience spellbound.

Some Yemenis speak a second language, and English is the most common one. Some older people also speak Russian because of the former connection between the Soviet Union and the PDRY. As a result of migrations, some African languages have reached Yemen.

Bargaining over grain at a weekly market is an exercise in eloquent Arabic and body language.

Long ago, people used to greet the imam by kissing the back and palm of his hand and the hem of his robe. Today, kissing the hand is an act of respect to the recipient.

BODY LANGUAGE

A Yemeni is almost as physically expressive as he is verbally expressive. When talking, Yemenis stand close together and look each other in the eye. It is quite common for members of the same sex to touch each other while talking. A man might clasp another's hand, or touch his shoulder. This is the Yemeni way of showing respect and affection.

People also use their heads and hands to communicate. Raising your eyebrows stands for "yes," while blinking both eyes at the same time means "no." To summon someone, join the fingers of the right hand and then, with the palm facing down, motion toward yourself. To ask a question, the thumb and forefinger are stretched out at right angles to each other, and the rest of the fingers are curled into the palm. Then the whole hand is waved back and forth. Even the position of the feet is important. Yemenis attach great importance to manners, so it is best not to point the soles of your feet at one of them because they consider this act to be extremely insulting.

MEDIA

Yemen's press is among the freest of the Arab countries. Despite paper shortages and interference from government officials from time to time, there are still hundreds of newspapers. Many of them are associated with political parties. The English-language *Yemen Times* is well known as a particularly vocal newspaper when it comes to criticizing government policies.

Yemen's mountains are gorgeous but they obstruct television reception. Despite poor reception, more television transmitters are being installed in mountain villages. Watching television is usually a family activity. In small villages, neighbors and friends often congregate in the few houses with television sets, or listen to the radio instead.

Yemen has two television channels, and programs are broadcast from Sana'a and Aden. For six days a week television can only be watched between 4 p.m. and midnight, when electricity is available. On Fridays there are programs in the morning before prayer.

Yemenis enjoy watching soap operas and comedy shows, many of which are filmed in Egypt or Syria. Sporting events are also popular, as are cartoons. The people are also interested in television coverage of their president and government officials. There are a number of locally produced cultural programs and the occasional documentary on Islamic issues or Yemenis overseas. The availability of satellite dishes is spreading fast, bringing Western television shows and news coverage to Yemeni homes.

A man reads the *Yemen Times*. This newspaper was created in 1990 by Dr. Abdulaziz al-Saqqaf. In 1995 he became the first Arab journalist to be awarded the International Prize for Freedom of the Press by the U.S. National Press Club.

ARTS

THERE IS A WEALTH of creative talent in Yemen and artistry is expressed in varied and colorful ways. Visually, Yemen is stunning. Fairy-tale style houses blend with dreamy landscapes. Urban mosques are endowed with exquisite decorations, illustrating the influence of the Islamic faith on artistic expression. The longstanding tradition of poetry reveals the spirit of the Yemenis, and their vivacious nature is depicted in wildly exciting dance and music.

POETRY

The Arab people had very little written tradition before Islam arrived, yet they still managed to develop a rich language of poetry to express their creativity. Instead of writing down a poem, it was memorized and passed down orally to the next generation. Poetry became a means of preserving a great body of history and tradition.

The Yemenis reserve one of the highest places in their culture for poets, who have played a part in shaping the course of events. The powerful words of the poet Mohammed Mahmoud al Zubayri helped to fuel the republican spirit during their struggle against the royalists. Contemporary poetry blossomed in the 1970s when poets of the new generation, who had not been part of the revolution, began to voice their opinions about the times and their dreams of the future.

Lively, witty poetizing is a popular form of entertainment, and Yemeni poets have perfected the art of spontaneous poetry. A poetry competition is a popular way to show off one's verbal talent and wit. At a wedding, the men from each family will often challenge each other with clever word play to entertain the guests. Satirical poetry, known as *hija* ("HEE-ja"), is also a favorite. One poet composes a verse and sends it to a second poet, who responds using the same meter and rhyme.

Opposite: **At one time, the dagger was used as a weapon, and its blade was very sharp. Today, these daggers serve mainly a ceremonial purpose.**

Not so long ago, tribal disputes were settled with guns instead of by "competing tongues." *Zamil* ("ZA-mil") is a genre of poetry associated with the tribes, and is still popular today. A tribal poet is the spokesman for the tribe; his poems are chanted by other tribal members while they march.

CALLIGRAPHY

Calligraphy is a beautiful form of writing, but more importantly to the Yemenis, it is an artistic expression of Islamic spirituality, and is used to decorate books and mosques.

Calligraphy is not just a case of writing the text; the design should be as full of emotion and ideas as the words themselves. The relation between the black letters and the white space around them produces a striking composition and conveys the true meaning of the written word.

By tradition, the pen used for calligraphy is made from reed or cane. Since calligraphy began when the Koran was first written, the pen is symbolic of the written word of God:

"And your Lord is the most generous,

Who has taught by the pen,

Taught humanity what it did not know."

Koranic inscription on the wall of a mosque in Shaharah. Calligraphers are masters of patience and concentration. Their art requires a serene atmosphere, removed from the constraints of daily living. Only in such a setting can a calligrapher's inner energy be conveyed to his writing.

YEMENI BOOK ART

There is ample evidence to confirm that Yemenis were masters of "book art." Several ancient manuscripts were discovered in the Great Mosque of Sana'a, some of them Koranic, others the remains of old documents and amulets. They were delicately calligraphed onto dried sheep or goat skin that had been specially prepared for writing. Although paper was known to the Muslims as early as the 8th century A.D., it was not until the 11th century that book production became common.

ARCHITECTURE

There is no doubt that great buildings and temples existed before the arrival of Islam. The province of Ma'rib, once the capital of the ancient kingdom of Saba, is a famous archeological site. Oral tradition describes a splendid palace called Ghumdan near Sana'a at the beginning of the Christian period, around the time of the kingdoms of Saba and Himyar. According to legend, the 20 stories of the palace towered above its surroundings, and each of the four sides was of colored stone: white, black, green, and red. It was said that bronze lions guarded the entrance to the palace and roared when the winds blew. The alabaster roof was so wafer thin that from indoors one could see birds flying over it.

Historians also confirm that there was an impressive cathedral in Sana'a, built around the same time as the Ghumdan Palace. This church, known as "al-Qalis," was made of teak and plated with gold and silver.

The arrival of Islam gave a new impetus to building. Just as Christianity inspired the Europeans to build cathedrals, Islam sparked its followers to build places of worship. Mosques were erected wherever there was a settlement. The Great Mosque of Sana'a, which was built in 630 A.D., is a wonder. Much of the material used to build this magnificent mosque was taken from older structures like Ghumdan Palace, and possibly from Sabean temples. Christian decorative motifs like pigeons, doves, and rosettes appear on the minarets and parts of beams. A remarkable feature of the Great Mosque is its wooden ceiling, which is inlaid with inscriptions and rich decorations.

The minaret of the famous Great Mosque. Notice the exquisite carvings on its outer walls.

A house built in the *zabur* style. Because stone is scarce in this arid region, clay is used instead as a building material.

THE ART OF HOUSE-BUILDING

In Yemen, a man's house is his castle. Great pride is taken in building it, and on completion, decorative calligraphic writing records the event on the exterior wall. The house styles in Yemen are unique, and regional variations have evolved over the centuries.

The reed houses in the Tihama villages are round or rectangular with a pointed thatched roof. There is a striking contrast between the simple exterior and the artistic interior. Colorful designs are painted over the entire ceiling, and the inside is decorated with beautifully carved wooden furniture. These reed houses look just like those found across the Red Sea in Africa.

In the coastal town of Hodeida, houses are built in the Red Sea style. These are multistoried, with Turkish windows and balconies, and they reflect foreign influence on Yemeni building styles.

The distinctive *zabur* ("ZAH-boor") architecture is common on the plateaus of the eastern and northern highlands. Here there is plenty of clay, but stone is scarce. To build a *zabur* house, horizontal layers of clay are placed one on top of the other, as though one were making a chocolate layer cake. The walls are coated with mud, but the layers are left visible. Parapets decorated with small arches adorn the roof edges.

Tall houses are also a favorite in the Hadramawt. The city of Shibam is often called the "Manhattan of the Desert," because it has over 500 skyscrapers, some of which are higher than 100 feet (30 m) above street level. Many of the Hadramawt houses are built from mud that has been sun-dried and made into bricks. After the walls have been built, they are plastered smooth with brown earth or light lime plaster.

DECORATION The Yemenis use intricate, geometric patterns painted in various color combinations to decorate their houses. The same patterns and motifs that women use to decorate their bodies are painted on walls, windows, doors, and ceilings, or carved into plaster and wood. The designs include zigzag lines, dots, floral designs, and date palm motifs.

On some houses, the windows are the most decorative element. The *takhrim* ("TAHK-rim") windows in Sana'a are well known. They look as though they were covered with lace because their alabaster panes are shaped into delicate patterns. The addition of colored glass makes them even more charming.

Doors and windows displaying skilled carpentry work remain as fine examples of the high quality work of Jewish craftsmen before their exodus. In the south, in cities such as Ta'izz, and in the Tihama, the influence of Indian workmanship can be seen in elaborate door carvings.

This glass window in the Rock Palace is a typical example of colorfully decorated windows in Yemen.

Inexpensive jewelry is sold at silver shops like the one above. The quality of some of the pieces compares well with European post-Renaissance jewelry and Ottoman and Indian court jewelry.

SILVERWARE

Arab women, like women elsewhere, have always been fond of jewelry. Traditional jewelry was made of silver, to local design. Sometimes colorful coral, amber, agate, glass, or ceramics were combined with the silver to create eye-catching pieces. The markets of Sana'a and Ta'izz are full of glittering head ornaments, necklaces, earrings, bangles, belts, and finger and nose rings. Finely crafted amulets, such as charm cases containing verses of the Koran, became popular after the arrival of Islam.

Yemeni Jews were master jewelers. When they emigrated from Yemen in 1949 and 1950, the imams realized that Yemen ran the risk of losing one of its most profitable crafts, so they decreed that before leaving, Jewish silversmiths had to impart their skills to Yemenis who remained.

Modern lifestyles have altered jewelry habits. Nowadays gold is popular among urbanites and less traditional jewelry is worn. However, for a special occasion such as a wedding, a bride is still always bedecked in the finest traditional jewelry.

DECORATIVE WEAPONS

Weapon making is one of the most valued crafts in Yemen. The distinctive curved dagger known as the *jambiya* is worn on a special belt by Yemeni men. Its design varies according to the region, the tribe, and the social standing of the owner.

The tribesman's dagger is called an *asib* ("as-EEB") and it has a bone or wooden handle. It is kept in a leather sheath and secured by a cloth belt. The *asib* is worn in the middle of the body, a sign of a free tribal warrior. The elite Qadis and Sayyids wear daggers known as *thuma* ("THU-ma"), which have a slender curve and ornate silver handles. These are kept in an embroidered or carved wooden scabbard.

In the past Yemen was renowned throughout the world for making high-quality steel blades. Today many of the blades are imported from Japan or Pakistan.

The hilt or handle determines the value of the *jambiya*, and its carving is a marvel of craftsmanship. The most precious *jambiyas* are those made of African rhinoceros horn, which takes on a rich luster with age. Once carved, the hilts are embellished with silver, and coins are frequently mounted on them.

In earlier times, the *jambiya* was sometimes encased in a silver filigree scabbard. Since this is extremely expensive, most scabbards are now made from special local wood. The craftsman carves two J-shapes from wood, and then hollows them to fit around the blade. The next step is to bind them together by using strips of goat skin. The dagger in its scabbard is then secured in place with a belt made of leather or finely woven cloth.

Making *jambiyas* is a very profitable trade, especially since male Yemenis start wearing them from the age of 14.

Top: **Yemenis of the Hadramawt celebrate the end of a harvest with a dance.**

Opposite: **Young or old, Yemenis love music.**

DANCING

Yemen has a longstanding and varied dance tradition. Each community has its own unique style of dance. There are dances that are intensely dynamic, and those that are more subdued. Some are light and airy, while others involve a lot of hopping about.

One of the liveliest dances is the *bara'* ("ba-RAH"), a style of dance that distinguishes one tribe from another. Each tribe has its own *bara'*, which is characterized by the number of dancers, the way they command their daggers, the steps, and the music. Only men perform the *bara'*, and always outdoors. It is danced during cooperative work projects, to welcome visitors, on festive occasions and national holidays, or simply when there is enough space to dance and people are in the mood.

In the northern highlands near Sana'a, as many as 20 men might dance the *bara'* to the beat of drums. Arranged in a horseshoe, the men watch the leader, an accomplished dancer, who stands in the middle and signals a change of step. The men start moving slowly, but the pace soon builds to a feverish tempo, with complicated whirling and intricate steps. Daggers carried in the right hand are used to "cut the air." A great deal of skill is required to coordinate arms and legs so that nobody gets hurt.

Lu'b ("li-BAH") is popular in parts of the highlands. The word *lu'b* means "to play," and as the name suggests, it is performed solely for entertainment. The dance is usually accompanied by love songs. *Lu'b* is often danced in pairs, and the partners are good friends or relatives. Sometimes men and women dance together, but this only takes place in the privacy of the family home.

MUSIC AND SONG

There is a rich variety of music in Yemen. In the cities, people enjoy the soothing sounds of the *oud*. The oud, which resembles a guitar, is a short lute. It often accompanies the lovely voices of solo singers. Along the Red Sea coast, musicians use it to play lively rhythms.

Besides the oud, many other instruments are used to produce the stirring sounds of Yemeni music. The *simsimiya* ("sim-sim-i-yah"), a five-string lyre, is popular in the Tihama, along with cymbals and the violin. There are also reed windpipes, which make high-pitched buzzing sounds, as well as a variety of drums. In the highlands, musicians beat the drums with their hands and often also sing.

Not surprisingly, Yemenis love to sing, and there are many songs for them to choose from: religious songs, poetry chants, and romantic ballads are some. In the past, military songs were very popular, particularly during the revolutionary 1960s. Iskander Thabit from Aden, whose tunes carried many political statements, is practically a legend in Yemen.

There are many popular Yemeni singers. One of them is Badwi Zubayr, a singer from the Hadramawt. People all over the Arabian Peninsula hum his songs.

CONTEMPORARY TRENDS

In recent years there has been an increased emphasis on preserving Yemen's cultural identity. Cultural centers have been established throughout the country to promote the arts, and tourism has also helped revive some traditional crafts. Traditional poems have been broadcast over the radio and recorded onto cassettes for everyone to enjoy. Two popular folk artists are the poet Shayf al-Khalidi and the musician Husayn 'Abd al-Nassar. Both come from Yafi, a mountainous region north of Aden, and work together to produce cassettes of poety. Their work has facilitated a "poetry exchange" throughout Yemen.

The variety of artistic expression is indicative of changing styles in Yemen. Contemporary folk art is thriving. One example is the design and manufacture of metal doors used at the courtyard entrance of houses. The design, colors, and complexity of the work display remarkable talent.

Modern painting has blossomed, and contemporary painters have embarked on a journey of exploration, painting brightly colored landscapes

AN ASPIRING PAINTER

Sabri Abdulkareem is one of Yemen's aspiring painters. He represents a new generation of Yemeni intellectuals who will influence the future of Yemen. This talented man is 36 years old. He works for the ministry of culture and tourism and belongs to the modern art group.

Much of Sabri's work has been inspired by his environment and reflects upon Yemeni heritage in architecture, poetry, and popular dress. Sabri portrays reality in a poetic way. Every color used in his paintings has symbolic meaning. For example, white is used to express sadness or purity while yellow represents death. Exhibitions have been held of Sabri's work; in a recent exhibition 45 paintings were displayed.

and portraits. The paintings of young artists like Sabri Abdulkareem are gaining popularity through public exhibitions.

Although most cloth is now imported, cotton and linen are still laboriously spun, dyed, and woven in certain regions of Yemen. The Tihama is known for its striped patterns. Natural dye from the indigo plant is used to create vivid blue and violet colors. In eastern Yemen, some garments are hand-embroidered with delicate patterns.

The Bedouin still weave sheep and goat wool into carpets. Leather goods, such as bags for carrying dates and water, are sometimes still handmade. Along the coasts, traditional patterns are woven from palm fronds into baskets, hats, and other useful items.

A Yemeni man shopping for an iron door, which is fast becoming a popular alternative to the traditional wooden ones.

LEISURE

THE YEMENI WAY OF LIFE involves plenty of social interaction, and exchange of news and gossip takes place during daily activities such as going to the mosque or the market. Yemenis also spend a lot of time with their families, thus much of their entertainment or leisure time revolves around the family.

GAMES

Yemeni children spend most of their time within the family and neighborhood either helping with the household chores or playing with friends. When they do have free time to play, older girls and boys usually have a younger brother or sister at their elbow. Boys tend to be more visible than girls. They are often seen huddling over a board game, such as backgammon or dominoes, in the street or marketplace. Other popular games that they play include cards and marbles.

Girls usually play closer to the home, and their leisure activities are often connected with home concerns and the Yemeni love of poetry. In the afternoon, while their mothers are out visiting neighbors, some girls might play with dolls while others make up their own games. They might sing, dance, and chant poetry. Sometimes the girls will pick a theme, perhaps beauty or cooking, and hold poetry competitions among themselves.

Some traditional children's games go back to ancient times and have been passed from one generation to the next. Unfortunately, few children play these games anymore. Other games and sports such as soccer have replaced them.

Top: **Dominoes is not just child's play. Adults often gather for a game or two.**

Opposite: **Children swinging after their household chores.**

TRADITIONAL GAMES

The Honest Person and the Thief (a traditional game for boys)
Participants: 5 or more
Equipment: 1 matchbox (in early days, this game was
played with a squared-off bone).

The players sit in a circle and take turns throwing a matchbox into the center. If the matchbox stands on its end, the thrower becomes "king." If it lands on one of the striking surfaces, the thrower becomes either "minister" or "soldier," based on markings made on the box or agreement beforehand. If the box lands on one of the broad sides, the thrower is declared "honest" or "a thief" (again based on markings made beforehand). The thief receives a "sentence" that is decided by the minister, supervised by the soldier, and agreed to by the king. The sentence might consist of doing situps or performing a service, such as making tea for the other players. Outrageous sentences are discouraged by the fact that any of the players could be the thief in the next game.

O Hillcock, O Hillcock (a traditional game for girls)
Participants: Any number
Equipment: None

Two lines of girls stand facing each other, stamping their feet to the rhythm of a song. Each team selects a girl who has a talent for spontaneous poetry. A theme is chosen, the first poet comes up with a verse around the theme, and then her team chants her words. The second poet retorts, and the game continues until one of the girls succeeds in silencing the other.

SPORTS

Soccer is a favorite pastime in Yemen. Boys always seem to be kicking a ball around, whether they live in a small village or the city. If soccer balls are not available, there is always a plastic bottle or a homemade rag ball that will suffice.

Sports are played on a part-time basis. There are very few professional athletes who compete internationally, but there are national league games in the cities. Yemen has competed in three Olympic Games but no participant has won a medal yet.

BATTHOUSES

A Yemeni proverb says, "The whole delight of this world lies in the hot bath." The public bathhouse is called a *hammam* ("HA-mahm"), and both men and women use them, although on different days. Yemenis love to go to bathhouses with friends. It is also a favorite place for a bride and groom to socialize separately with friends and relatives before a wedding.

Inside the bathhouse, the hot rooms offer the bathers a place to chat with friends or do a couple of exercises. If the room is not too crowded, a group might perform a Yemeni dance, while others sing songs.

Once bathers have had enough heat, they proceed to wash themselves. Sometimes they might ask a friend to help them. This is a great act of friendship. When the bather reaches the changing room, the others will say "*hammam alhana*" ("HA-mahm ul-HA-na"), which means "a pleasant bath," to which the polite reply is the same Arabic expression.

Not all Yemenis can afford to take frequent dips in bathhouses. This man just washes himself at a well.

MEN'S GATHERINGS

Chewing qat is an expensive habit. It is possible to tell how well off a man is by the quality and quantity of the qat he chews.

The afternoons are quiet in many towns because men often attend qat parties, which may last for as long as four hours. The parties take place in the *mafraj* of a house, and everyone takes turns hosting it. The custom is to bring your own qat. Information about where the gathering will take place on a particular day is exchanged in the market or at the mosque.

Since Yemenis love verbal banter and jokes, the afternoon parties usually begin with the exchange of good-natured insults and jokes. Afterward, weighty subjects such as politics, business, religion, and the economy might be discussed in smaller groups, or in pairs. Important business decisions are sometimes made at these gatherings. Quite often poetry is composed and recited. On a special occasion there might be dancing, music, and singing. But there is usually some quiet time at the end of the gathering for enjoying the view or simply for meditation.

Yemenis chew qat when there is company, and at important occasions like weddings and funerals.

WOMEN'S GATHERINGS

Yemeni women are not as restricted as women in other Arab countries, such as Saudi Arabia. However, most of their activities take place within their home or neighborhood. In the afternoon, many women attend neighborhood gatherings. In cities such as Sana'a, women put on their best clothes, makeup, and jewelry to attend what are known as *tafritah* ("ta-FREE-tah") circles.

Tafritah takes place in the *mafraj* of one of the women's houses. At a *tafritah*, the hostess passes around glasses of sweet tea and bowls of raisins, popcorn, or nuts to nibble on. A few of the women may chew qat. These gatherings offer women a chance to relax, exchange news, and discuss family issues with other women of the neighborhood. They may also listen to music and dance. From time to time, some of the older women will tell stories.

Young girls often accompany their mothers to adult gatherings. Usually they sit and listen quietly to the conversation. This gives them an opportunity to learn about the lives of Yemeni women of all ages.

FESTIVALS

YEMEN HAS SEVERAL religious and secular holidays that bring its people together at certain times of the year.

RELIGIOUS OCCASIONS

Friday is a day of public prayer and the official rest day when government offices are closed. Every Friday Yemeni men try to offer their midday prayers in the mosque, where a religious leader delivers a special sermon.

Prophet Mohammed's birthday is honored by Yemenis. This is a quiet day that reminds worshipers of their Islamic faith and duties. At home, parents might read stories about Mohammed to their children.

Like Muslims in other countries, Yemenis also celebrate Mohammed's death. On this day, they remember his ascension to heaven. In some areas such as Sana'a, men and children spend the day visiting their female relatives.

Left: **Men praying in the courtyard of a mosque.**

Opposite: **Musicians help intensify the festive wedding mood with their lively performance.**

Some Muslims study the Koran more frequently during the month of Ramadan than at any other time of the year.

RAMADAN AND FASTING

The Islamic month of Ramadan is the ninth and most sacred month of the Islamic calendar. On the 29th day of the eighth month, Yemeni Muslims look toward the western horizon for the new moon. If it can be seen, Ramadan begins with the sunset. If not, Ramadan will begin the next day. The month is set aside for fasting to commemorate Allah's revelations to Mohammed.

Muslims fast because Allah has commanded them to do so. A fast heightens spiritual awareness and brings one closer to God. Those who are ill or on a journey during the month of Ramadan do not fast but should make up for the days lost.

During Ramadan, a drummer wanders through the streets in the early hours of the morning to wake the neighborhood by beating his drum or chanting in a loud voice. Yemenis rise, eat a small meal, and then they fast for the rest of the day. The biggest meal of the day is consumed after a cannon sounds at sunset. There is a special diet for this meal, including many nutritious foods such as soup, meat or cheese, fresh fruit juices, milk, dates, and figs. Sweets are eaten more than usual to give the body energy and are offered to friends and relatives who visit in the evening. Children often carry a colorful lantern with a candle inside when making their rounds of visits.

In the second half of Ramadan, it is a tradition for children to march around the neighborhood singing songs. They stop at houses to collect nuts, sweets, and donations.

FEASTING

The appearance of the new moon signals the end of Ramadan. At last, fasting is over and it is time to celebrate *Eid al-Fitr* or the celebration of the breaking of the fast. *Eid* is a time to give thanks to Allah. There is an official public holiday with no school or work for at least four days.

During the *Eid*, children dress in special clothes bought to be worn only on this day. After breakfast, there are congregational prayers in the mosques and visits with relatives. Children are then given some money and candies, and everyone eats a hearty lunch.

The *Eid al-Adha*, or the feast of the sacrifice, is another holiday. It starts on the 10th day of the month of the pilgrimage, and is the highlight for those who have made the *hajj*. This holiday commemorates Abraham's obedient willingness to sacrifice his son to Allah, and many families sacrifice a lamb, which symbolizes giving oneself to God.

On the first day of *Eid al-Fitr*, the whole family gets up early and has a light breakfast either at home or at a food stall like the one shown here.

109

SECULAR HOLIDAYS

In recent years, the official activities and functions that mark the Day of National Unity have taken place at a different city every year. This is to foster a national spirit among Yemenis.

In spite of unification, Yemenis still observe some of the public holidays observed by the two earlier Yemens. The extent of the celebrations on these holidays depends on the region.

Revolution Day is celebrated in the south on October 14. This commemorates the day that the National Liberation Front (NLF) launched a revolution against British rule in South Yemen.

The final withdrawal of the British and the subsequent formation of an independent state, which later became the People's Democratic Republic of Yemen (PDRY) under President al-Shabi, is celebrated on November 30, as Independence Day.

Northern Yemenis celebrate their Revolution Day on September 26, the day when a group of military officers led by Colonel Abdullah Sallal overthrew the ruling imam in North Yemen and established the Yemen Arab Republic (YAR).

Labor Day recognizes the contributions of Yemeni workers to the country's economic development. Although New Year's Day, according to the Gregorian calendar, is not a particularly important day for Yemeni Muslims, with increasing Western influence, parties are held in some of the larger hotels.

OFFICIAL SECULAR HOLIDAYS

January 1:	New Year
May 1:	Labor Day
May 22:	Day of National Unity
September 26:	Revolution Day
October 14:	Revolution Day (sometimes called National Day)
November 30:	Independence Day

DAY OF NATIONAL UNITY

The most significant modern event in Yemen was the end of national division and the establishment of the Republic of Yemen. For this reason the Day of National Unity, celebrated on May 22, is the most important secular holiday for Yemenis.

In the week preceding the holiday there may be discussions in school about the importance of this day. On the actual day schoolchildren parade through the streets carrying the national flag and singing the national anthem. There are also military parades, traditional dancing and music, and sports events such as camel races and soccer games.

Every year the president makes a stirring speech highlighting Yemen's economic and social progress. The speech is broadcast over television and radio.

Drummers beat the rhythms of the street parade to celebrate the important Day of National Unity.

In the ancient Middle East, the date palm was a symbol of beauty and victory. The date palm motif decorated temples, palaces, city gates, and the crowns of kings.

AGRICULTURAL FESTIVALS

Long ago the Yemenis used astronomy as a guide to mark the seasons for planting. One of the most important stars in Yemeni tradition, Sirius, the Dog Star, is the brightest in the sky. In July, the dawn rising of this star signals the arrival of the late summer rains that have been, and still are, so important to farmers for irrigation purposes. Planting, harvesting, and the two rain periods became a time of great rejoicing.

In some regions, ancient traditions are kept alive. Every September Yemenis and tourists flock to the area of Jawf in the al-Mahra governorate, which borders Oman, to see the autumn festival. The festival is reminiscent of an ancient festival of that region that celebrated the end of the first monsoon rains.

Farmers share in the bounty of nature by enjoying themselves. During the festival, there is folk dancing and music, as well as sporting events like camel races and tug-of-wars. Festival celebrations usually conclude with a public banquet.

HARVESTING DATES

Deification of the date palm began in pre-Islamic times, and since then, many festivals have been held during harvest time in mid-July. In the 14th century the arrival of fresh dates was celebrated with a holiday in the town of Zabid, located in the Tihama. Ibn Battuta, who visited Zabid in the 14th century, described the festival: "The people of this city hold the *subut al nakhl* (feast) in this way—they go out during the season of the coloring and ripening of the dates to the palm groves on every Saturday. Not a soul remains in the town, whether townfolk or stranger. The musicians go out (to entertain them) and the bazaar folk sell fruit and sweetmeats. The women go out riding on camels in litters."

WEDDINGS

A wedding in Yemen is a joyful occasion and is often celebrated over a number of days. The marriage ceremony consists of signing a contract in the presence of the *Qadi*, an Islamic scholar of the law, who will recite the first *sura* of the Koran. The bridegroom's father then throws a handful of raisins on the ground, symbolizing a happy future for the couple. Everyone present tries to gather as many raisins as they can.

Weddings in Sana'a are usually celebrated in a big way. The butchers arrive early in the morning to prepare meat for the feast. If the family can afford it, several sheep, and even a calf, will be bought for the meal.

When the groom arrives for the meal, he is accompanied by dancing and singing men. The bride arrives a little later with her father. It is customary for the women of the neighborhood to climb onto the roof of the house, where they welcome the newlyweds with high-pitched singing.

Top: **A bridegroom in traditional headgear.**

Left: **Men dancing with their *jambiyas* during a wedding celebration. In Sana'a, a tradition has emerged in which the groom and other men drive to the edge of the Wadi Dhahr, a fertile valley of small villages, on a Friday morning to dance. Sometimes several wedding dancing parties go on at the same time.**

FOOD

IT IS A YEMENI CUSTOM to offer food generously. Guests are treated as royalty, and the host will always say, "Come in and have what there is."

The cuisine is extraordinarily varied in Yemen. Each region has traditional specialties and every tribe has a distinctive cuisine. Many dishes are made from local ingredients and flavored with numerous spices. Some of the spices used were introduced by the ancient caravan trade and came all the way from Indonesia and India.

Opposite: **A shopkeeper selling fruit and nuts in a market.**

YEMENI CUISINE

On the whole, the diet is simple and nourishing, making use of locally grown grains such as sorghum, millet, and corn, and flour made from legumes. Fruit and vegetables are added to the diet, varying across the country depending on how fertile the land is. Sometimes Yemenis eat chicken and mutton, particularly if there is a special occasion like the birth of a child, when guests come to dinner, or when a person is ill and is believed to need richer nourishment.

Islam has an influence on food and drink. Muslims do not eat pork or drink alcohol. The Koran advises that pork is unclean.

LOCAL HONEY

The Yemenis are fiercely proud of locally produced foodstuffs, known as *baladi* ("BAHL-a-di"), which means "of the country." Such products are believed to be superior in quality to foreign foods. Yemenis purchase them whenever they are available.

Locally produced honey is a delicacy that is in great demand. It is an essential ingredient in many traditional recipes. Even a slight variation from the local flavor is an indication that the honey is impure. Honey is also a status symbol and is frequently given as a gift. Some of the most expensive honey in the world comes from the Hadramawt region. Honey also has a medicinal use in Yemen—it is eaten to treat stomach ailments.

Top: **The skillful cook stretches the dough by tossing it in the air while his bread bakes in the mud oven.**

Opposite: **Meat on sale is very fresh as animals are slaughtered on the spot.**

THE KITCHEN

A traditional kitchen is a rather stifling place. It is dark because the windows are kept closed to prevent dust from getting into the food. When the cooking fires are lit, the kitchen can become unbearably hot.

Every kitchen has at least one *tannur* ("TANN-ur"), a cylindrical clay oven. *Tannurs* come in all sizes, and women say there is a real knack to breaking in the cook for *tannur* baking. What they mean is that it takes a while to get accustomed to the heat of the *tannur* so that one can slap the bread on the insides of the oven. Young girls get lots of practice on the smaller *tannurs* before they progress to the larger ones.

There is a little hole at the bottom of the *tannur* where bits of fuel, such as charcoal or wood, are put in. When food needs to be grilled or boiled, a grate can be placed over the top opening, and the food placed on it.

Besides the *tannur*, most kitchens are equipped with charcoal braziers to keep coffeepots warm. Many urban homes have gas stoves.

The conventional refrigerator is quite an invention. It consists of an alcove in the wall with wooden doors. A big jar of water sits inside. The outside wall has holes, so that when the wind blows through them, evaporation cools the water in the jar and keeps the food fresh. Sometimes when the women are bored, they will peer through the holes to see what is happening in the streets.

For washing up, there is a kitchen sink, which is a shallow trough on a ledge leading to an outside drain. If the kitchen does not have a tap, water will be collected and stored in great earthenware jars.

Cookware is stored on shelves above the oven. There are aluminum saucepans, stone pots, and plenty of bread baskets. Spices and herbs hang in baskets on the walls. There are rolling pins for dough, pestles for crushing grains, and hand mills to grind corn or pepper. Scissors are used for just about everything—from cutting vegetables to removing the legs off a chicken.

FOOD PREPARATION As soon as the men leave the house, the women get busy cooking and cleaning. Radio music plays continuously in the background, and women chat with family members as they go about their daily tasks.

Many activities take place in the kitchen. There is little counter space, so women often prepare food on trays while kneeling on the floor. To make bread, dough is stretched across a stone and then slapped against the walls of the piping hot *tannur*. While bread is baking, a broth or stew might be simmering in a clay pot. Meanwhile, with their fingers or a wooden spoon, someone will prepare *hilbah* ("HUHL-bah"), a dip for bread. *Hilbah* is uncommon in rural areas but it is a favorite in the cities. Tangy tomato, garlic, and red pepper sauces are mixed by hand or in an electric blender. Bread is dipped into these sauces.

Fried fish makes a good snack. It is usually sold at the entrance to the fish markets.

MEAL PATTERNS

The day starts early with the dawn prayer. After prayer, some Yemenis have something light, such as tea and a bit of bread. Others wait until 8 a.m. when they eat breakfast. This consists of scrambled eggs or cooked beans, along with bread or porridge.

Lunch is the biggest meal of the day in Yemen. If guests are invited, they eat with the men first, followed by the women. Otherwise the whole family eats together. Lunch in Sana'a might start with a few radishes dipped in a fenugreek sauce to whet the appetite. Then comes the wheat or sorghum porridge, or a cold pancake with a hint of mint or thyme, to satisfy the hunger pangs. A vegetable stew, potatoes, beans, and plenty of bread and *hilbah* ensure that even the heartiest appetite is fully satisfied. Unlike in Western meals, where meat is served during the main course, in Yemen meat is always served at the end of a meal.

For those with a sweet tooth, dessert could be fresh fruit, a caramel pudding, or a hot, flaky pastry with honey. After the meal, tea and coffee are served in another room, where people can relax and the men can chew qat.

For most people supper is a simple, light meal that the women prepare after the sunset prayer. Supper often consists of the day's leftovers, perhaps chicken or eggs with tomatoes, bread, and water. After supper, some men set off for the mosque for the fifth and final call to prayer. After the evening prayer, the men return home to spend time with their families.

TABLE ETIQUETTE

It is a Yemeni custom to share food generously. When offered food, one should accept graciously so that the host is not offended. As elsewhere in the Middle East, refusing food usually means one of three things: the guest feels the host cannot really afford to be so generous; the food is unclean or not prepared properly; the guest does not like the host. Turning down food is a social blunder and an insult to the host.

Yemenis eat their meals while sitting on the floor, rather than at a table. The food is served in metal pots, stone dishes, and china bowls, and carefully arranged on a colorful plastic cloth. Before they eat, they have to wash their hands. The Yemenis do not use knives, spoons, or plates. Instead, everyone eats from communal dishes, taking the food from the part closest to them. Meat and vegetables are scooped up with bits of bread or the right hand.

Yemenis never eat or offer food with the left hand since this is reserved to wash themselves after visiting the toilet.

FAVORITE FOODS AND DRINKS

Every community has its favorite fare. City folk enjoy fruit, honey, vegetable stews, salads, and rice. Along the coast, people eat fish. The tribal people love their own local porridges, which are highly nutritious.

Bread is to Yemenis what pasta is to Italians. Every day the women of the household will bake enough bread for breakfast, lunch, and supper. There are all types of breads, and most are made from local grains. *Khubz tawwa* ("KU-butz tah-WAH") is ordinary bread that is fried at home, and *lahuh* ("LAH-huh") is a festive pancake made from sorghum. In the cities, modern bakeries sell oblong *roti* ("ROH-tee") loaves. The word *roti* was introduced a long time ago by Indians who traded in the port of Aden.

The national urban dish is *saltah* ("SAHL-tah"), which means soup. The favorites are lamb or thick lentil soup with vegetables such as beans.

Beans are loved by both Muslims and Jews. A Yemeni proverb says, "When I have Yemeni broad beans, my time is a happy one." A Jewish saying goes, "Broad beans are indispensable for the Sabbath."

Bread and fruit are the staple foods of Yemenis. Unleavened bread is served at all meals. When fresh, it is delicious, but if left for more than half a day, it has the texture of a tough rag.

SALTAH

lamb or chicken stock
1 cup finely chopped boiled lamb or chicken
1 cup boiled lentils or beans
1 egg, beaten
1 tablespoon chopped coriander leaves
1 recipe quantity of *hilbah* (see below)
1 cup boiled rice/potatoes/wedges of flat bread

Boil the lamb stock then add chopped meat and vegetables. Thicken the soup with a well-beaten egg. Then add coriander leaves and bring to a boil again. Put the *hilbah* mixture on top and serve immediately with rice, potatoes, or flat bread.

Hilbah

$1/4$ cup ground fenugreek
2 tablespoons chopped garlic
3 tomatoes, chopped
$1/2$ cup chopped onions
$1/2$ teaspoon salt
a small pinch of turmeric, saffron, cardamom, and caraway seeds

To make *hilbah*, pour a cup of boiling water over fenugreek and let it steep for three hours. Drain off the water, beat fenugreek with garlic, tomatoes, onions, salt, and spices.

Sometimes a refreshing green yogurt soup called *shafut* ("SHA-fuht"), made with sour milk mixed with chili beans and herbs, is poured over bits of bread and eaten in the afternoon.

A typical dessert is *bint al-sahn* ("bint al-SA-han"), a sweet bread made from eggs. This is dipped in a mixture of butter and honey.

The world-famous Yemeni coffee from the port of Mocha is not as commonly drunk as tea because it is more expensive. Instead, people drink a flavorful brew known as *qishr* ("KU-shir"). The drink is made from ground coffee husks and ginger. For those who prefer a stronger coffee, there is *bunn* ("BUN"), a traditional coffee made straight from the beans. For Yemenis the perfect end to a meal is tea in small glasses, usually very sweet, and sometimes flavored with cardamom or mint.

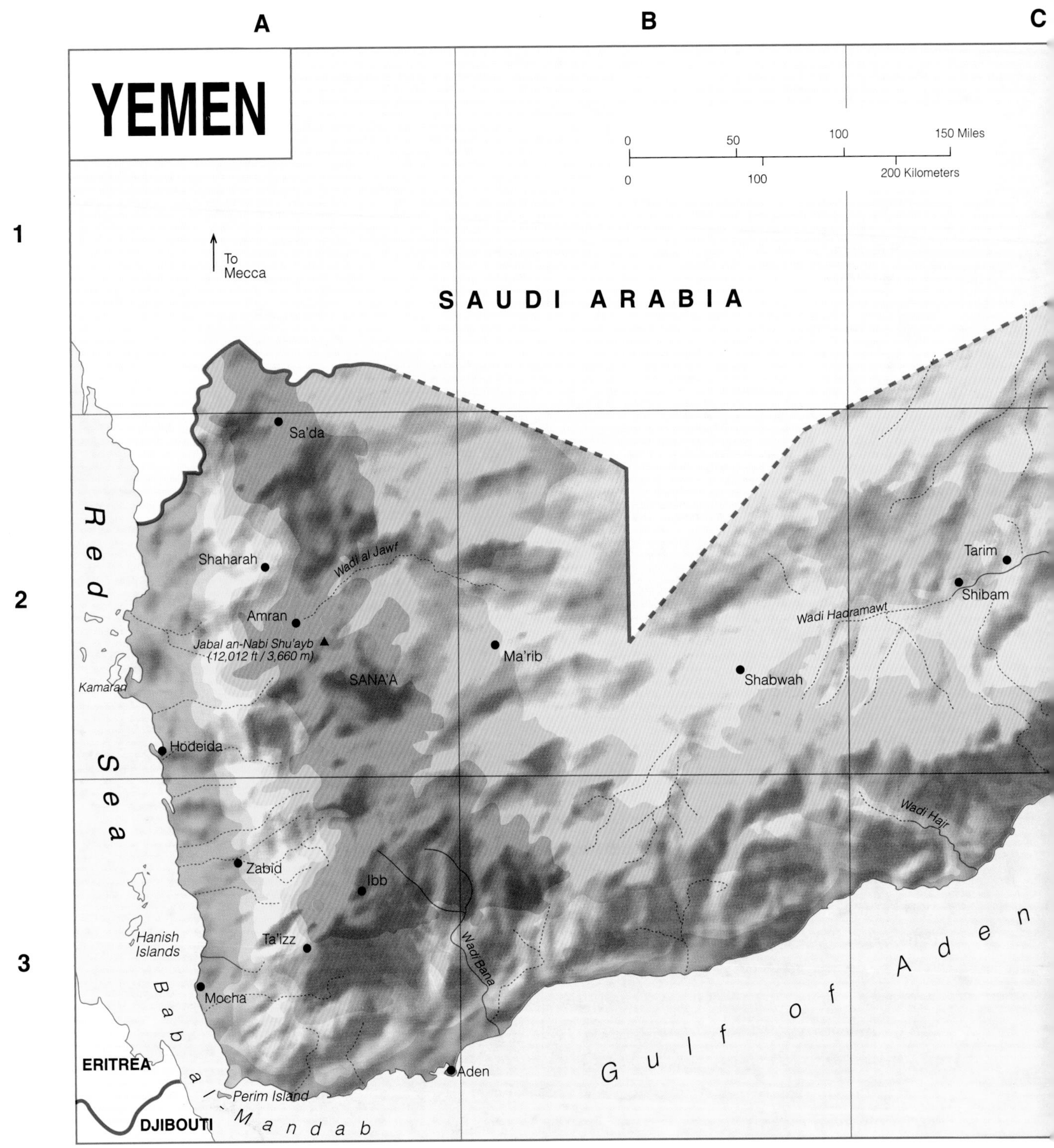

YEMEN

0 50 100 150 Miles

0 100 200 Kilometers

1

To
Mecca

SAUDI ARABIA

Sa'da

2

Red

Shaharah

Wadi al Jawf

Tarim

Amran

Wadi Hadramawt

Shibam

Jabal an-Nabi Shu'ayb
(12,012 ft / 3,660 m)

SANA'A

Ma'rib

Shabwah

Kamaran

Sea

Hodeida

3

Wadi Hajr

Zabid

Ibb

Wadi Bana

Hanish
Islands

Ta'izz

Gulf   of   Aden

Mocha

Bab   al   Mandab

ERITREA

Aden

Perim Island

DJIBOUTI

D

OMAN

Mahrat
Mountain

Wadi Rakhawt

Wadi al Masilah

N

Socotra

Same scale as main map

● Capital city
● Major town
▲ Mountain peak

Feet	Meters
16,500	5,000
9,900	3,000
6,600	2,000
3,300	1,000
1,650	500
660	200
0	0

Aden, A3
Amran, A2

Bab al-Mandab, A3

Djibouti, A3

Eritrea, A3

Gulf of Aden, B3

Hanish Islands, A3
Hodeida, A2

Ibb, A3

Jabal an-Nabi Shu'ayb,
  A2

Kamaran, A2

Ma'rib, B2
Mahrat Mountain, D2
Mocha, A3

Oman, D1

Perim Island, A3

Red Sea, A2

Sa'da, A2
Sana'a, A2
Saudi Arabia, B1
Shabwah, B2
Shaharah, A2
Shibam, C2
Socotra, D3

Ta'izz, A3
Tarim, C2

Wadi al Jawf, A2
Wadi al Masilah, C2
Wadi Bana, B3
Wadi Hadramawt, C2
Wadi Hajr, C3
Wadi Rakhawt, D1

Zabid, A3

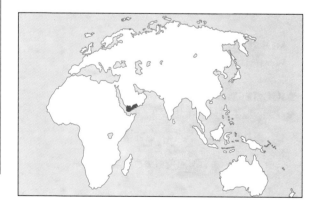

QUICK NOTES

OFFICIAL NAME
Republic of Yemen
Arabic: Al-Yaman

CAPITAL
Sana'a

POPULATION
16,600,000 people (1997 estimate)

MAIN CITIES
Aden, Ta'izz, Hodeida

PORTS
Aden, Hodeida, Mocha

GOVERNORATES (PROVINCES)
Abyan, Aden, al-Bayda, al-Jawf, al-Mahra, al-Mahwit, Ataq, Dhamar, Hadramawt, Hajjah, Hodeida, Ibb, Lahji, Ma'rib, Sa'da, Sana'a, Ta'izz

ISLANDS
Socotra, Perim, Kamaran, Hanish Islands

LAND AREA
214,230 square miles (554,856 square km)

MOUNTAIN RANGES
Western and Central Highlands

HIGHEST POINT
Jabal an-Nabi Shu'ayb (12,012 feet/3,660 m)

FLAG
Red, white, and black horizontal stripes

NATIONAL EMBLEM
The eagle, a symbol of strength and liberty of the nation

MAIN EXPORTS
Crude oil, hides, coffee, vegetables, dried fish, cotton

MAIN IMPORTS
Textiles, manufactured consumer goods, petroleum products, cement, machinery, chemicals, foodstuffs

CURRENCY
Yemeni Riyal (YR)
YR 136.66 = US$1

NATIONAL LANGUAGE
Arabic

MAJOR RELIGION
Islam

IMPORTANT HOLIDAYS
Day of National Unity (commemorating the establishment of the Republic of Yemen) —May 22
Eid al-Fitr and *Eid al-Adha*—dates are decided by the lunar Islamic calendar

POLITICAL LEADERS
President: Lt-Gen. Ali Abdullah Saleh
Vice-President: Maj-Gen. Abd ar-Rabbuh Mansur Hadi
Prime Minister: Dr. Abdul al-Karim al-Iryani

GLOSSARY

bara' ("ba-RAH")
Tribal dance with variations in the steps and the number of dancers.

Eid al-Adha ("id ul-ah-DAH")
Feast of the sacrifice that marks the end of the pilgrimage to Mecca.

Eid al-Fitr ("id-ul-FIT-r")
Celebration of the breaking of the fast at the end of the Islamic month of Ramadan.

futa ("FOO-ta")
Gathered calf-length skirt worn by Yemeni men.

Hadith ("ha-DEETH")
The collection of Prophet Mohammed's sayings that supplements the Koran in guiding Muslims.

hajj ("HAHJ")
The Muslim pilgrimage to Mecca.

imam ("ee-MAHM")
Muslim religious leader.

jambiya ("JAHM-bi-yah")
Curved dagger.

Koran ("koh-RAHN")
The holy book of Islam.

mafraj ("MAHF-rahj")
Living room, usually on the uppermost story.

muezzin ("MWEHZ-in")
The mosque official who announces the hour of prayer.

oud ("OOD")
Musical instrument similar to a lute.

PDRY
People's Democratic Republic of Yemen.

qat ("kaht")
Plant whose leaves are chewed for relaxation.

Ramadan
The Muslim month for fasting.

Shari'ah ("SHAHR-i-a")
Islamic law.

sharshaf ("SHAHR-shahf")
Loose, black cloak worn by Yemeni women.

sheikh ("SHAYK")
Tribal leader.

sitara ("SEE-tahr-a")
Brightly colored cloak worn by Yemeni women.

suq ("SOOK")
Traditional marketplace.

tannur ("TANN-ur")
Cylindrical earthenware oven.

tafritah ("ta-FREE-tah")
Women's gathering, usually in the afternoon.

wadi ("WAH-dee")
Dry riverbed filled in rainy seasons.

YAR
Yemen Arab Republic.

BIBLIOGRAPHY

Hansen, E. *Motoring with Mohammed*. Boston, Massachusetts: Houghton Mifflin, 1991.

Johnson-Davies, D. *Desert Fox Seif bin Ziyazan*. Dokki, Cairo: Hoopoe Books, 1996.

Khalidi, M. *Queen of Sheba*. London, England: Hood-Hood Books, 1996.

Mackintosh-Smith, T. *Yemen: Travels in Dictionary Land*. London, England: John Murray, 1997.

Serjeant, R.B & R. Lewcock. *Sana'a: An Arabian Islamic City*. London, England: Scorpion Communications and Publications, 1983.

Yemen in Pictures. Minneapolis, Minnesota: Lerner Publications, 1993.

INDEX

INDEX

INDEX